TEMPTED BY HOLLYWOOD'S TOP DOC

BY
LOUISA GEORGE

MILLS
BOON

This book is sold subject to the condition that it shall not, by way of trade or otherwise, be lent, resold, hired out or otherwise circulated without the prior consent of the publisher in any form of binding or cover other than that in which it is published and without a similar condition including this condition being imposed on the subsequent purchaser.

® and TM are trademarks owned and used by the trademark owner and/or its licensee. Trademarks marked with ® are registered with the United Kingdom Patent Office and/or the Office for Harmonisation in the Internal Market and in other countries.

First published in Great Britain 2016
By Mills & Boon, an imprint of HarperCollins*Publishers*
1 London Bridge Street, London, SE1 9GF

Large Print edition 2016

Special thanks and acknowledgement are given to Louisa George for her contribution to The Hollywood Hills Clinic *series.*

ISBN: 978-0-263-26128-8

Our policy is to use papers that are natural, renewable and recyclable products and made from wood grown in sustainable forests. The logging and manufacturing processes conform to the legal environmental regulations of the country of origin.

Printed and bound in Great Britain
by CPI Antony Rowe, Chippenham, Wiltshire

Having tried a variety of careers in retail, marketing and nursing, **Louisa George** is thrilled that her dream job of writing for Mills & Boon means she gets to go to work in her pyjamas. Louisa lives in Auckland, New Zealand, with her husband, two sons and two male cats. When not writing or reading Louisa loves to spend time with her family, enjoys travelling, and adores eating great food.

Books by Louisa George

Mills & Boon Medical Romance

Midwives On-Call at Christmas
Her Doctor's Christmas Proposal

One Month to Become a Mum
Waking Up With His Runaway Bride
The War Hero's Locked-Away Heart
The Last Doctor She Should Ever Date
How to Resist a Heartbreaker
200 Harley Street: The Shameless Maverick
A Baby on Her Christmas List
Tempted by Her Italian Surgeon

Visit the Author Profile page
at millsandboon.co.uk for more titles.

To my Zumba buddies Jackie, Sue,
Roisel, Yenny and Avril.

I can't think of a better way to start the day
than dancing and having fun with friends.

I'm very lucky to have you guys in my life.
Thank you xx

**Praise for
Louisa George**

'I recommend this read for all fans of medical
romance reads who love a good and sweet,
tender romance with a bit of a feisty streak and
crackling tension.'
—*Contemporary Romance Reviews* on
200 Harley Street: The Shameless Maverick

'*The Last Doctor She Should Ever Date* is a
sweet, fun, yet deeply moving romance. This
book just begs to be read and I would definitely
recommend this book and any other ones
written by Louisa George to all contemporary
romance fans.'
—*Harlequin Junkie*

'A moving, uplifting and feel-good romance,
this is packed with witty dialogue, intense
emotion and sizzling love scenes. Louisa
George once again brings an emotional and
poignant story of past hurts, dealing with grief
and new beginnings which will keep a reader
turning pages with its captivating blend of
medical drama, family dynamics and romance.'
—*Goodreads* on
How to Resist a Heartbreaker

CHAPTER ONE

'LOLA! WHERE ARE YOU? Lola!' The sing-song screech came from inside the trailer.

Outside the trailer, Lola Bennett came to a halt and took a long calming breath. When that ran out she took another one. And…

So, it seemed calm would be eluding her today.

Behind her she heard muttered grumbles between the director, the assistant producer and the leading man. Irrational though it was, she felt guilty that the woman who employed her was ramping up the film budget and delaying filming because of mild stomach cramps, no doubt brought on by an overdose of her large kale and wheatgrass breakfast smoothie.

Lucky, Lola told herself. *Dream job. Steps to the stars. Foot in the door…*

Phooey. Being personal assistant to A-lister Cameron Fontaine was probably some poor misguided soul's dream job, but for Lola the constant demands were fast turning into a nightmare. Sometimes she thought the waitressing job had been preferable…but then all she had to do was look around her and breathe in the hallowed Hollywood air, see the actors going over their scripts—scripts like the one she was working on—and feel the shiver of excitement course through her. And she knew she was exactly where she wanted to be: Los Angeles. She was here, finally here. The only place on earth where she could achieve her crazy, wild dreams. The City of Angels.

All would be well, if only Cameron Fontaine could be remotely angelic. Once? Too much to ask?

'Lola!' Clearly there was nothing wrong with Miss Fontaine's vocal cords.

'Yes, Miss Fontaine?' Lola swung open the trailer door, letting the heavily perfumed air—a perfect blend of cedarwood, frankincense, sandalwood and lemon balm aromatherapy for clarity and focus today—disperse enough for her to enter without risk of asphyxiation. Then she took a risk and stepped in, with her usual fixed smile. It would all work out well. *Smile and work. Smile and work.* 'Hello! I hope you're feeling better? Here's the paracetamol you asked me to get. And your single-shot decaf latte with cashew milk.'

'You are such a honey.' The leading lady lay on the white leather couch, a hand at her brow, and gave a *brave me* smile. Lola had seen her working on that particular grimace in her large gilt bathroom mirror more than once. 'Tell me, sweetie, what's the gossip from the set? Are they panicking yet? I'll bet that old maid of a director is sweating. Tell them I'll be out soon. I just need to get my strength back.'

'Maybe you should eat something solid, rather than just juicing?'

'You're joking, right? I have to get into this teeny costume every day for the next few weeks.' Cameron mopped at her forehead with the back of her hand. 'And get hold of that doctor...what's his name? Kim? Get him on the phone. Tell him I need to see him again.'

'Oh?' Maybe Cameron really was sick, instead of acting or just plain attention-seeking? Before taking this job, Lola had seemingly been the only person in the whole world who had had trouble trying to work out the difference between her boss's award-winning talent and her award-winning time-wasting. She'd stopped short of calling her a diva, but that didn't stop the glossies naming her as one. Having got to know her a little more, Lola was reframing Cameron as a hardworking actress with high standards, who wasn't afraid of asking for what she wanted. She could learn something from that. Although the diva did sometimes take centre stage. 'Of course. Yes. I'll get him right away.'

First, she cracked the seal on a fresh bottle of mineral water and poured it into a glass tumbler.

'Lola, what are you waiting for? Phone him.'

'I'm getting you a drink so you can take your tablets. Let's get them into your system and starting to work.' It was going to be a very long day, and Lola would be very glad when she fell into bed later with a good book to whisk her away from the reality of her life. Which hadn't turned out exactly how she'd hoped. No studio had optioned her script, no director had even read it so far. More than once she'd thought about returning home to London…but she needed to give herself a fair chance here, not risk the humiliation of going home and admitting she'd not just failed, but lied to her family too. And, God knew, even though some days she hated it, she needed to keep this job to pay the exorbitant rent on her shabby apartment. And eat. 'Would you like me to get the studio nurse? She's here and available, and I'm sure she wouldn't mind—'

'A *nurse*? A nurse? Honey, I'm award-winning. I need a *doctor*. I need that Kim doctor.' And with that Cameron closed her eyes. Conversation over.

Lola observed her for a few seconds. It didn't need any kind of medic to see that the actress was in fine health. Her blonde hair shone, she was beautifully pink, breathing normally with a small secretive smile on those camera-ready lips. But Lola was nothing if not dutiful. She pulled out her phone and dialled.

'Hello!' She'd been briefed by Cameron to always converse with a smile in her voice. 'Is this The Hollywood Hills Clinic? Yes? Great! I have Cameron Fontaine here and she needs to see the doctor. Wait, I'll just ask.' Lola cradled the phone to her shoulder and whispered, 'Is it an emergency, Miss Fontaine?'

A perfectly plucked eyebrow rose on a serene, pain-free face. 'It depends what they mean by emergency. *I* would like to see a doctor—so, yes, they should act quickly.'

'But is it a matter of life or death?'

'I suppose…' A reluctant pout. A dramatic pause. 'Not really.'

'Are you dying, Miss Fontaine?'

'Oh. No. No. Of course I'm not *dying*. But don't tell them that, obviously.' Cameron sat up elegantly and straightened her space desert warrior costume, putting little strain on the perfectly honed abdominal muscles that had been on the front of every magazine last month as she'd *frolicked* in the waves in Hawaii—while Lola had been left in LA to supervise a spring clean of Cameron's Bel Air home, take the dogs for grooming, organise a lunch for fifty for Cameron's return…*yada, yada…*

Lola sighed—inwardly, of course—and spoke to the receptionist. 'Please ask him to come as soon as you can. Thank you…I will, yes.' Lola passed along the message. 'The doctor will be here soon. He's in the middle of a surgery, but will pop over when he's finished.'

'Pop over. You're such a sweetie. Say it again…' Cameron gave a real smile now. 'Say it again.'

'Pop over.'

'Pop! Oh, my, I do love your English accent. Just heavenly. Teach me?'

'Yes! Of course!' Clearly, whatever ailed Miss Fontaine would have to wait. But Lola had no doubt that the pain would resurface at exactly the same time as the doctor.

'Excuse me, Dr Lewis, there's another call for you.'

'Another one? Not now,' Jake Lewis barked across the OR at his surgical assistant. 'I told you, I don't want to know until I've finished here.'

'But it's the studio. They won't—'

'Not now.' Jake sucked in the antiseptic air and steadied himself. Refocused on his patient, a nineteen-year-old quarterback with a diagnosis of type-two neurofibromatosis: an incessant ringing in his ears, increasing left-arm numbness and a sudden penchant for falling over. All pointing to a large tumour on his vestibular nerve, which had been confirmed by scans.

With enough luck and Jake's skill, the boy might well be able to catch and pass a ball after this surgery. He would, hopefully, also be able to hear again—although, he might not. He would also probably never fulfil his lifelong dream of playing at a high level in the NFL. The disease process was slow, but there wasn't always a great prognosis long term. This kid's future was on the line and someone wanted Jake to see an actor about, what—an irritating cough?

And, yeah, maybe he was being an assumptive ass, but in his experience there hadn't ever been a need for a neurosurgeon on a film set during the normal day-to-day scheduling. Emergencies—yes. But this wasn't an emergency, they'd said so already. The first time they'd called. And the second…

The assistant hesitated, the phone still in his outstretched hand. 'But…they…you…'

'Didn't you tell them last time? If it's an emergency they need to call 911 and I'll meet them in the ER, otherwise I will be there as soon as I've finished this complex neurofibroma surgery. If they don't understand what that is, explain, in words of less than two syllables, that I'm a brain surgeon, and ask them to guess what I'm busy with right now.'

When James Rothsberg had head-hunted him

for his Hollywood Hills Clinic it had been the biggest boost to Jake's career, the opportunity to work with the very best California had to offer. And it had promised a decent living with money to spare to pay back his parents every cent and more for the sacrifices they'd made for him. Money, too, to pay for healthcare for his father's failing health.

That they wouldn't accept a dime from him was another issue altogether, along with the fact that even though Jake worked in one of the best hospitals in the state, his father refused to set foot through the door. Not that it stopped Jake from trying. Again. And again.

But the job came with the proviso that he'd fill in when necessary on the clinic's film studio roster. In extremis. And Dr Kim's sudden and necessary absence due to family problems meant they were in extremis. He'd have to live with it, along with all the tender egos who demanded nothing less than a qualified doctor to apply a plaster.

'Okay, everyone. Back to work, concentrate, this is the tricky bit. We have to...' he manipulated the probes '...isolate and expose the tumour… There it is… Pretty tough guy, this one, will take some clever dissecting…'

Three hours later, after a distressing conversation with his patient's parents, when he'd tried to be as honest and hopeful as he could about the boy's future, Jake pulled into the film studio, showed his security pass and was directed to the set.

Seriously? His whole life he'd been working towards neurosurgery and now, just because one of his colleagues was away, he was here. In… The spool of annoyance on repeat in his head jerked to a stop. He looked around. Stared. *What the hell?* Outer space? The set was a mock-up of a crashed spacecraft on a sandy planet. All around him were creatures with three eyes or two heads and, strangely, holding very Earth-like guns… Plus a lot of cables that could easily trip someone up, and a few worried-looking humans huddled around a large film camera, watching something on a screen.

'Hey?' He stopped a man carrying a ladder as he walked by. 'Cameron Fontaine? Where can I find her? I'm the doctor. She rang, more than once, to request my assistance.'

'In her trailer. *Again*. Out there, take a left.' The man pointed wearily across the set and beyond. 'Biggest trailer, you won't miss it. Do us a favour and wave a wand, bring her back? They're all going nuts here.'

Jake wandered through the set and out into a car lot where there were around a dozen trailers. One, in the far corner, was very definitely, pointedly, larger than the others.

'Excuse me? Can I help you?' A very cross English voice, out of place in…outer space…had him spinning round. The owner was another angry-looking human with wild fiery red hair that appeared to match her bad humour, and a smattering of freckles in a pale complexion. It was the frown that stood out most, though.

'I'm looking for Cameron Fontaine. She called for me. I'm Dr Lewis.'

'You're the doctor? But you're not Kim. She usually sees Kim.'

Believe me, lady, I don't want me to be here either. 'Dr Kim is away at the moment. I'm the fill-in. For the duration of filming.' But he'd be having words with James when he eventually got back to the clinic. Surely someone else could do this? Someone less busy, less qualified, someone who actually cared about all these Hollywood theatrics?

The woman in front of him shook her head and the mass of red curls bobbed around her shoulders. Man, her hair was shiny, and she had dark chocolate eyes that were huge and…condemning. She was wearing a top that was a similar colour to her eyes. And why he even noticed that he had no idea. Standard issue black skinny jeans clung to… No, he wasn't going there. He was not going to look at her and assess her attractiveness like everyone else in this city where looks were king. No doubt she was just the same kind of blinded-by-the-lights airhead wannabe actress. She was pretty enough. Not like the tall willowy brunettes that breezed in and out of his life, but there was something about her that set her apart. A fragile beauty.

So, okay, he had a quick peek and she had a damned fine body. Curves. Something you didn't see often around here. Nice curves.

And a disappointed glint in her eyes that made him feel as if he'd let her down. 'Well, that's just perfect. Brilliant. We've been waiting for you for hours and everyone's starting to get very grumpy and for some reason it's all my fault and you're not even the right guy.'

'Whoa.' It was fine for him to feel bummed out about this, but no way was it okay for her to join in. 'I can leave right now, if you prefer. I have plenty of real patients to keep me occupied.'

'No. No. No. Stay right there. You'll have to do. The director's getting on my back, Cameron won't go outside, and we all need her seen as soon as possible. Please.' Her eyes narrowed for a moment. Then she seemed to pull herself together. Smacking her lips, she clasped her hands in front of her as if steeling her nerve. She found him a smile. It wasn't terribly convincing, but it was there. 'Sorry. I'm Lola Bennett, Miss Fontaine's PA.' He could have sworn she also uttered the word 'dogsbody' under her breath, but he couldn't be certain.

'Jake Lewis. Neurosurgeon to the stars. Apparently.' He stuck out his hand.

Which she took in hers and gave a short firm shake. Her hand was warm and petite and just touching it gave him a weird jolt through his skin. She looked down at where their hands touched, then back at him with a question in her eyes. Then she blinked. 'Okay! Well! Let's do our best, shall we? Miss Fontaine's trailer is right here. Be warned, though, she may not be exactly chuffed to see you.'

'Chuffed?'

'Sorry, I mean pleased. Delighted. English, you see. As in I'm from England… Obviously you speak English too…just a different sort…' And then she smiled for real, the chocolate eyes blazed and her mouth curled into a pretty curve. Which had a very strange but real effect on his cardiac rhythm as he followed her into the trailer.

He put it down to the whole bizarre scenario, the extra-terrestrial vibe, the raised blood pressure caused by harassment during complex surgery. The drive through relentless traffic. It was nothing to do with the very talkative Lola Bennett, of that he was sure.

'Hello!' There was a forced joy to her voice that was just a little panicked as they stepped into the trailer, and for a fleeting moment Jake felt sorry for her. 'Miss Fontaine? The doctor's here!'

'About time too. Kim? Oh, Kim, I'm so glad—' The beautiful blonde actress Jake had seen on billboards around town and on movie screens countless times sat up and glared. 'You're not Kim.'

Lola was by her side in a second, talking as if to a small child, eagerly soothing and endlessly optimistic. 'No, Miss Fontaine, this is Dr Lewis. *Jake*. He's here to see you. Dr Kim is away at the moment.'

'Well, bring him back. I can't see...' she waved her hand at Jake as if shooing away an irritating dog '...Jack here.'

'It's Jake,' Lola said smoothly, as she offered a silent apology to Jake in the form of a shrug and a roll of the eyes. 'He's from the clinic, so he's bound to be good. Excellent, I'll bet.'

Unable to take this fawning any longer, Jake stepped forward. 'Miss Fontaine, I'm Dr Kim's stand-in. There is no question of bringing him back. What's the problem?'

'I can't discuss it with you. Kim knows every-thing.'

'Oka-a-ay. It'll be in your notes then? I'll remote-access them from here.' He put his lap-top bag on the table next to her and unzipped it. Pulled out his computer and fired it up. 'Please be assured that I am bound by the same confidentiality as Dr Kim. I am as capable as he is.' *If not more so. And more highly qualified.* 'If you can just tell me what's wrong, then we can try to fix it.' *Soon.* And, yes, he realised his tone was just a little annoyed. But he had very sick patients, a young man with his whole future in doubt—his whole life—and instead of being where he was needed, he was here. Doing this.

The actress began to shake and blink quickly. 'What's wrong? What's wrong? I need health advice and I have the wrong doctor in my trailer, that's what's wrong. Please go. Now. I won't see anyone but Kim.'

What the hell? 'I can assure you—'

'It's Kim or no one.'

'Then it'll be no one. He's not going to be back for months—'

'So go.'

Jake bit back a curse. 'I came all this way and you won't even let me talk to you? Just like that?'

'Just like that. Now go.' And with a final flourish she flung herself back against the cushions and closed her eyes. He presumed this meant that the consultation was over.

'Sorry to have wasted your time,' he growled, not sorry at all as he slammed down the laptop lid, snatched up his bag and stalked out of the door. Wasting *her* time? Wasting her time? His fist curled around the bag handle as he strode back towards the set. What a joke. He was definitely going to talk to James about this.

'Dr Lewis? Jake? Wait, please.' That English accent again. He swivelled on his heel. Lola was standing at the bottom of the trailer steps, wringing her hands. 'How about I find you a cup of tea? Would that help?'

'I doubt it. It certainly won't get me the last hour of my life back.'

'But it might help to sit for a while. Calm down before you head back into the traffic.' She looked at her watch. 'It's almost rush hour, it'll be a nightmare.'

'I think I've just had one already. Tell me I'm going to wake up soon.'

Lola raised her shoulders. 'She has a habit of changing her mind.'

'So do I. From right this minute. I'm not coming back. I'm not surgeon to the stars.'

'She may ask to see you again. Soon. Like in five minutes.'

'I'll be busy. With patients who actually want my input and expertise. I have better things to do with my time than pander to hypochondriacal celebrities.'

But for some reason he couldn't really understand, he followed Lola towards a truck dispensing snacks and drinks and waited until she'd ordered two English breakfast teas. Tea—the great soother of tempers, according to the Brits. No serial or costume drama was ever made where the mention of tea didn't happen at least twice. He hated it.

Then, taking the tray of drinks, he let her lead the way to a marquee and a plastic table and chair set-up. Lola looked dejected while desperately trying not to appear so. 'I'm so sorry, Jake. Can I call you Jake? Or do you prefer Dr Jake? Dr Lewis?'

'Jake's fine.'

'She's a bit temperamental, she's spent her life telling people what to do. And they do it. Just like that.' She clicked her fingers. 'I'm guilty of doing it too—but, then, I get paid to. She'll come round, you just have to let her calm down and think logically.' She bit her bottom lip, gave a conciliatory smile that lit up her eyes and whispered, 'She will, eventually.'

'Whatever she pays you isn't enough. Leave. Get another job.' So it was curt, but damn…how could Lola let her boss talk to her like that?

The smile and the light vanished. 'I'm sorry?'

'It's not healthy to be around self-obsessives. Actually, it's really not *worth* it. Just because you want to be noticed, a career in Tinsel Town, right? She's your ticket? Actress, right? Like all the others who come here because they want the bright lights. It's not worth it, Lola. Find another job. That kind of person will suck you dry, drive you mad.'

Now Lola frowned, eyes wide. 'And this is your business because…?'

Good question.

He didn't usually make assumptions and feel the need to sort someone else's life out. In fact, he usually steered as far away as possible from involving himself in anyone's life. Particularly women's. The only thing interfering had ever achieved was a damned headache, and sent out a message that he cared…or was interested…or wanted to commit. He wasn't. He didn't. 'I'm just saying, there are better careers than being someone's assistant or a Z-list actress. Most don't get very far anyway, it's only the top tiny percentage who can make a living at it. If you want my opinion—'

'Actually, I don't. But thanks for making my day a whole lot worse.' She stared at the steam rising from her tea, then stirred two packets of sugar into her cup. Which was refreshing, because most women he knew in this city would rather have eaten dust than sugar. It was the new axis of evil…or something. She looked dejected, and there was a simmering behind her eyes that signalled danger.

There was also a cloud of coiled anger hanging over them and, if he was honest, it was probably due to him. He'd started off this whole debacle in a lousy mood and things had got worse from there. If she was right and Cameron did ask him to return, it would help if he smoothed things between them. Plus, he didn't want word of this to get back to James, who was insistent that all patients be treated with kid gloves…and that was usually Jake's mojo. The patient came first—always. But also…and this was the weirdest thing… he felt bad at adding to Lola's troubles. He'd seen a glimpse of her smile and, strangely, he wanted it back again.

'Lola—'

'Oh? There's more? Which part of me do you want to pick apart now? You've done my job and my pathetic-sounding future—how about you move on to my face or my body?' The joy in her voice had been replaced with irritation. The happy bounce that had seemed to live in her bones—gone. Yes, she was pissed at him. Very. No one ever spoke to him in that tone, and there were flashes of gold sparking in her eyes now. It was…well, it was all very interesting. She leaned forward, waving her teaspoon at him. 'You don't know the first thing about me but somehow think you can storm in here and give me life advice?'

'Er…' He began to explain. 'It's—'

But she jumped right on in. 'Well, seeing as we're handing advice out so liberally today, let me give you some, Dr High and Mighty. I don't care who you are or what qualifications you've got, you don't get to condescend me as if I am worthless. And you don't get to make assumptions about anything I do or who I am. Okay? I was trying to be nice to you because she can be a bit of a B-I-T-C-H. And I totally understand how you can be angry with her for being a diva too—and now I've said it and I promised myself I never would—because she is a very good actress and she can be thoughtful sometimes. Rarely, but it does happen.

'I thought a cup of tea and a chat would help because in my experience they usually do, but you know what? Forget it. There are plenty of doctors in Los Angeles who would give their right arm to be here in this privileged position, doctors who care. Who want to help. Who are actually nice. So I'll go phone one of them, shall I? I think we're done here.'

And with that she scraped her chair in the gravel and stood. Her previously pale face was now a bright beetroot red. The sunny smile a mere figment of his memory. And to his chagrin, he realised Lola Bennett had done what no woman had ever done to Jake Lewis—she'd brought him to a point where he had to chase after her and grovel.

CHAPTER TWO

'LOLA.'

God give me strength. Some days she really, *really* wanted to change her name. She hesitated on her path back to the trailer, slowed and then stopped, wishing her burning cheeks would cool down. The doctor may well be dashing and delicious to look at with his cropped dark hair and startling blue eyes, and so what if he had a body that the leading man on set would die for? Jake Lewis was a pompous jerk in a suit and she didn't want him to think he'd got the upper hand.

But he was the only doctor here so she needed to be nice to him because finding another one might take another couple of hours. And she was pretty sure Cameron would change her mind, *again*, and insist on seeing a doctor before the day was out. So Lola was stuck between the two of them trying to find a happy place. 'Yes? What now?'

Dr Lewis's lips twitched at the corners, but he kept his distance. 'You didn't finish your tea.'

'I don't want it any more, thank you.' She tried to keep the irritation out of her voice, she really did, but it shone through regardless.

He stepped forward and beckoned to her. 'But I'm told on good authority that it might help. And it's going cold.'

'So?' She stuck her hands on her hips and waited for his apology.

'So, they're going to clear it away if we don't go back.' The jerk jerked his head towards the canteen seating area. Two forlorn cups sat on the empty table. And, God, she was parched. With all this running around she hadn't had a chance for a drink in ages. Dr Lewis just carried on as if an apology was the furthest thing from his mind and that he hadn't just insulted her every which way he liked. 'Come on, come back and finish it before they take it away.'

But no way would she sit with him again until— 'No, Jake, I'm waiting for an explanation.'

'I see.' The twitch at the mouth turned into a thin line as he pondered her words. He really was very lovely to look at—but, then, so was everyone in LA, even the set carpenters were beautiful and always screen-ready. It was like living in a magazine or on an episode of Entertainment Daily.

This guy, though, he had an arrogance that shot through the better-than-good looks, a haughty jaw and a manner she didn't particularly understand—it was as if he really didn't want to be here. Who wouldn't want to be surrounded by all this wonderful Hollywood chaos?

She tapped her foot. 'Still waiting...'

'Ah. Well, I haven't ever waited tables, Lola, but I think it generally works like this: when customers leave a table—or rather *stomp* away—it indicates that they've finished and it's okay to clear their used cups away.'

'Too clever for your own good.' She couldn't help the smile. 'And I didn't stomp.'

His gaze ran from her face, down over her body and lingered a little at her backside. Which made her face heat even more. Her stomach suddenly started with a strange fluttery feeling and she wondered if she was coming down with the same thing as Cameron.

He nodded. 'You so did. Little angry stomps.'

'Condescending too? Great.' He'd been watching her that closely? 'Well, it's hardly surprising given the circumstances. And I meant I'm waiting for an explanation of why you were so rude.'

'Oh.' He gave a small shrug. 'That.'

'Yes. That. An apology would be nice.'

He actually looked surprised, as if saying sorry was something he'd never ever thought about, let alone done. But he walked back towards the table and she felt intrigued enough to follow him. She just about caught his words, more of a mumble really. 'I apologise if my words upset you.'

'Not sorry you said them. Not sorry you jumped to conclusions. You're just sorry I was upset? Where did you learn the art of apologising?'

'You're supposed to learn it? Is that what they teach in British schools? The art of apology?' He stood at the table while she sat down—no doubt a play for power. 'Figures.'

'By which you mean?'

He lifted his cup to his mouth and took a sip. Grimaced. Put it back down again. 'Look, things got a little heated back there. I think we need to start over.'

Hallelujah. Because she didn't dare face Cameron and admit she'd scared the doctor away. Even if he did deserve it. 'Yes, yes, we do.'

'Excellent. First things first.' He turned and walked over to the café truck, chatted briefly with the chef—even laughed! Laughed. The man had a sense of humour...but clearly had no intention of sharing much of it with her. Then he returned with a steaming cup of coffee. He sat, sipped and smiled. 'Great. Now, where were we?'

'You don't like tea?'

'No.'

'So why didn't you say anything before?'

'You ordered and assumed I'd want it. I was being polite. It is possible.' He leaned back in his chair and smirked. 'I admit, I was an idiot.'

Still no *I'm sorry*. Interesting. 'To be honest, Cameron can be difficult. I have to bite my lip an awful lot.' She didn't tell him about how she screamed into her pillow when she was so frustrated and utterly exhausted by her demands, or had fantasised about a jellyfish attack on that Hawaiian beach, while she had been knee deep in doggy-do with three over-excited, totally over-pampered Chihuahuas at the grooming salon.

An eyebrow peaked. 'So why do you stay?'

'Have you tried to get a job here, with everyone else all vying for something in the industry? She pays reasonably well—although it's long hours. And because she's the closest I've got to a film director since I arrived here. That's my target, really. The longer I'm with Cameron the more I'll meet the right people. I need her. I need this job. I know that sounds mercenary, like I'm using her, but I really need the contacts and exposure. Does that make me a bad person?'

He looked at her for a moment or two, and again she felt a strange rising sensation in her stomach, a need to look away but a compulsion to keep staring into those bluest of blue eyes. 'Lola, I don't know you, but from what I've seen so far I couldn't imagine you're a bad person. A little full on, maybe—'

'My dad says I'm a chatterbox.'

'I'm not commenting on the grounds that I may incriminate myself further.' But he gave a wry smile in agreement. 'Basically, you're just doing what everyone else does—feathering your own nest. Making things work for you. It's the way of the world. It's why I'm here instead of back at the clinic, or back in Van Nuys, where I grew up. Networking, making connections. How are you going to get on in life if you don't use your contacts?'

Well, that certainly made her feel a little better. Although he'd clearly given it a lot of thought and justified it all down the line. Was he one of those true workaholic types? Or was he just completely self-focused?

She'd met a lot of people like that here—really, she'd thought she was highly ambitious, but her over-achieving tendencies paled into insignificance compared to those of some of the men she'd met. The ones who had stood her up because of a last-minute audition and hadn't bothered to call her and had left her sitting in a bar, like a lemon. Or who had used their in-between-jobs actor badges to repeatedly make her pay for everything on dates. Or—the very worst—the one who had slept with her as a way of getting to meet Cameron. That one had really stung. She'd fallen heavily for that guy and all he'd wanted had been an introduction to her boss.

Her love life had taken a serious dive since she'd moved here, and now she was totally off dating anyone. Definitely. It was going to be just her and her scripts and, she thought with a sigh, Cameron and her three little Chihuahua babies.

Having drained his coffee, Jake gave her a small smile. 'So you're an actress, then?'

'No. God, no. Although I did study drama from being about three years old and did my time on stage at university, but I fell in love with words, creating characters. Making things up. I'm a writer. Screenplays.' What a buzz to say that out loud. Finally...*finally*! She'd escaped the endless expectations and was chasing her own dream, instead of being forced to live someone else's. Although, she realised, freedom did come at a price—guilt, mostly.

He sat upright. 'And you came all the way from England just for that?'

'*Just?* People have done things that are far more rash. I wanted to be part of the scene here. This is where screenplays get made into movies. This is where someone can take my work, my idea, and make it a reality. Besides, my dad's from LA and he always talked it up.'

'So if he liked it, why did he leave? I presume he left?'

'He met my mum and married her and they

moved back to her home, which is London. Basically, he gave up his career here for love.' He'd taken second best for a job, moved countries, given up dreams. She was not going to follow in his footsteps—she was going to mould her own. Chase her *own* dreams. Hard.

She wasn't going to give anything up for love— when she was ready she was going to have it all. She just wasn't sure if she would ever be ready— how did you know? Her plan was to achieve all those things her father hadn't. To be a success. Because when he'd watched his daughter performing on stage all she'd seen in his eyes had been the light of regret. Lola never wanted to have any regrets. Or to walk on a stage ever again.

Jake looked startled. Shocked. As if the whole idea of love was alien and somehow absurd. 'Why would anyone would do that? Why take a chance on something that could just as easily fall apart? What does he do now?'

'He teaches drama, which he loves. And I'm sure he's happy where he is. I know he adores his family. Too much at times. But he used to tell such amazing stories about living here and the films he was in. Did you see *Big City Drive*? No?

It was about life in LA in the eighties. He said it was really accurate. The whole city vibe. I think I fell in love with this city just from that film. Although it does help that my dad was in it.'

Jake gave her a look that made her think he didn't much like it at all. 'And how's it working out for you?'

She couldn't look him in the eye and lie, so she spoke to the air around them. 'It's going just fine. Great! Look around you—isn't this brilliant? Over there is Alfredo Petrocelli, the best director in the world, as far as I'm concerned. And I'm breathing the same air as Matt Ringwood and Cameron Fontaine—although her air is usually infused with some weird aromatherapy combinations depending on her mood, and they change—a lot. But, all things considered, it couldn't be better.'

'And yet your body language says the opposite.' Those blue eyes narrowed a little. 'Tell me the truth, Lola. It's not all glitz and glamour, is it?'

Why did this man make her feel simultaneously nervous and yet eager to talk? How did he read her so well in the space of…what? Half an hour? She wanted to brush everything off with a big happy shrug but, well, she was a little sick of lying about how much fun it all was and how wonderfully exciting it was, when really sometimes she felt so despondent she wanted to cry. She was lonely. She was poor. She wasn't making the right connections quickly enough. She was running out of money. She couldn't bring herself to show her script to anyone. It was bad enough that she had to lie every time her father phoned.

But, then, she didn't know Jake from a bar of soap, so why should she spill her guts to him? 'It's fabulous, actually. You should see Cameron's house in Bel Air. It's amazing. And she has great parties.' Which Lola organised completely but had to keep a 'low profile' for. No partying for the assistant, just background work creating the illusion that Cameron had done it all on her own. 'Really. Fabulous. Now, I think I should probably be going.'

Jake frowned. 'Where? Back to Cameron? Won't she yell if she needs you? That seems to work.'

'Yes, she will. But I do have other things I should be doing. Besides, she needs me to go over her lines.'

But he didn't seem to want to move, so she was kind of stuck here, being polite. Although that wasn't too much of a hardship. After the initial bad beginning, things had started to smooth out a little—largely, she mused, due to her never-ending search for the positive in things, which was starting to falter a little.

He leaned back and crossed his legs. From what she could see of them they were toned, strong, clothed in expensive fabric. A dark suit, very professional. In fact, from this angle she could see the stretch of linen across his chest, the bunched muscles in his arms. He clearly did more working out than lifting a scalpel. And that was so none of her business. She looked away—only this time it was at his face.

His eyes met hers again and she felt a shiver of something strange as he said, 'So, what's it about, then, your screenplay?'

Wow. The first person to actually ask.

She'd prepared her elevator pitch, she knew exactly how to sell it to a director or producer in one sentence. Perhaps she could try it out on him?

'Lola! Lola!'

No such luck.

She gave him a little nod. 'See. I have to go. But, please, don't disappear on me, she's probably—'

'*Lola!*' The pitch was high, the voice wobbly.

'Oh, she really does sound upset. Maybe you should come too?'

'Okay. Sure. Once more unto the breach and all that…' He closed his eyes for a second and then breathed in deeply, as if summoning up courage. 'Do we need hard hats?'

For a moment Lola felt as if she had an ally. Everyone else took Cameron so seriously it was nice to share a confidence. She laughed. 'Only if she throws something at you.' At his worried grimace she laughed again. Harder. 'She has terrible aim. She hasn't actually hit me yet.'

Jake watched as Lola again clothed herself in her positive jolly guise and entered the trailer. For a few seconds she'd let him see past that façade to the real woman—she was an interesting character. Clearly driven, if not a little spirited. Still, there was nothing wrong in chasing a dream. She was articulate and had a self-deprecating sense of humour, which was infectious.

She almost ran over to Cameron and Jake had a suspicion that there was some affection there for her boss despite what she said. 'Hey, are you okay? What's the problem?'

The actress wiped tears from her cheeks. 'I don't know. I feel…well, I don't feel right. I'm so…out of sorts.'

Jake stepped in. 'Are you in pain anywhere, Miss Fontaine?'

'No. Not pain exactly.'

Great. Not helpful. 'Can you describe what this *out of sorts* feeling is? Is it anywhere in particular? An ache? A stabbing pain? Nausea? Headache? Dizziness?' It was like playing lucky dip.

'No.' Tears fell faster.

'She was nauseous earlier.' Lola looked from one to the other as if that was the complete answer.

'It's gone now, I'm just a little upset. Something I ate, no doubt.' Cameron sighed. 'But I don't think I'll be able to do much today. Lola, honey, can you tell them I won't be out for the rest of the day?'

Lola frowned, but quickly wiped it from her face. Her voice was soothing, soft and positive.

'Maybe you're just a little over-tired? You've been working very hard recently with only one little break in Hawaii. That wasn't enough—you need to make sure you book in a longer break between shoots next time. I'll put it in your diary.' While she talked she brushed Cameron's hair back from her face and held a glass of water out for her to drink. 'I think they're on their break now, anyway. They've been doing some stunt rehearsing to fill in—Matt's big fight scene, you know what a perfectionist he is, so don't worry, everyone's fine about it. How about we see how you feel in a few minutes? Perhaps Jake could give you a tonic or something?'

A tonic? Did people still have those? He was all clued up on brains and, after his stint in ER as an intern, could manage most emergencies. But general non-specific malaise? He wasn't sure about that. He knelt in front of Cameron.

'Perhaps Lola could excuse us while I examine you?' He shot a hopeful look at Lola and she nodded.

'Great idea. Let's make sure we're not missing anything.'

'No. No. That won't do at all. Please, just give

me a tonic. Something…something non-toxic. Oh, I don't know, maybe just water? Would more water help?' Cameron put a protective hand to her stomach, although Jake thought it was an odd subconscious action.

Then his mind began to join the dots. General malaise. Nausea disguised as a stomach upset. Hand on abdomen. Tears. *Non-toxic.*

She's pregnant. She's pregnant and she doesn't want anyone to know. 'I'd really like to talk to you in private, Cameron. Just talk. I won't examine you if you don't want that.'

The actress looked at him for a good long beat. She gave a minute shake of her head, her eyes wide and a little scared. Clearly, anyone finding out about this, even her assistant, was a big deal. But didn't she know she needed to take care? To eat the right things? Did she know for sure or just suspect? Did she have an OB/GYN?

Miss Fontaine sat up and patted her cheeks with a tissue. 'You know what? I'm actually starting to feel a bit better. Perhaps a little more water, then I'll go back outside. Get some air. Maybe we could do some sitting-down scenes to conserve my energy.'

Jake wasn't convinced. 'Cameron, are you sure you don't want me to look you over? Or I can arrange for someone else to come see you? This evening? To your home if you want?' *An OB/GYN? Midwife?* He gave her a studied look, hoping she could read through his words. Trying to maintain confidentiality with someone else in the room was difficult. 'I could call someone.'

'No. Thank you. You've been very attentive. But I'm fine. Absolutely. You can go.'

He fished into his bag and drew out a card, which he gave to her. 'Here's my personal cell number. Call me any time.'

For the first time since he'd met her, Cameron smiled. 'Thank you. You're very kind.'

Just concerned. 'Any time. Okay?'

Then he nodded to Lola to come outside with him. Thankfully she followed until they were out of hearing distance.

'Thank you, Jake. I think all she needs is a bit of reassurance. You know what these people are like—they get very anxious about their bodies—it's so important to them to be perfect. Obviously.'

Yes, well, he still wasn't happy about the situation. He was on a set with a presumably pregnant actress who was at all kinds of risk. However, he also had to remember that pregnancy was a perfectly natural and normal state. 'I think she needs to rest when she's feeling tired. If there's no pain or…anything else, she can continue to work. I've got to go back to the clinic and check on my patient from this morning, but I'll come back later. Just to double-check she's feeling okay.' And to convince her to seek further advice. Somehow.

'Thank you, that's very kind.'

'It's not, it's just routine.'

'But you could have just walked away. Thanks for putting up with us. I'll see you later. If they're filming when you get here, just pop on over to the trailer. That's where I'll be, no doubt. That is… well…you know. If you want. We could wait…in there. Or…sorry, I'm rambling. Bye.'

As Lola smiled he felt momentarily as if his breath had been sucked out of his lungs. She turned and walked back towards the trailer and he realised he was waiting for the angry little stomps. He kind of missed them.

She was all kinds of confusing. She didn't take any rubbish from him, but she took it from her boss. She stood up for herself in some situations, but not in others. She was hard working and committed. And she was, surprisingly and refreshingly, genuinely nice. Lola was the only real thing here—the rest was fabrication and fairy tale.

And he realised, as he climbed back into his car, that he wasn't thinking about coming back to see Cameron at all. It was her assistant that had him looking in the rear-view mirror for one final glimpse.

That was a danger sign if ever he knew one.

CHAPTER THREE

THE HOLLYWOOD HILLS CLINIC was bustling as usual, regardless of the time of day or night. After checking on his patient, Jake took the lift to the management suite and walked along the bright corridor, his footsteps tapping on the marble tiling. It was a far cry from the well-intentioned but underfunded public hospital he'd worked at prior to the phone call from James that had promised to change his life.

It had. And, he hoped, working here had made his parents' lives easier. For too long they'd scrimped and saved and sacrificed for their only son to achieve dreams way beyond any they'd dared to have for themselves. And every once in a while he took a breath and appreciated how very different things could have been for a relatively poor kid from Van Nuys; at least now with his handsome salary he could make up for all of their sacrifices. Even if he couldn't make up for the effect those sacrifices had had on his father's health.

He rapped on the door and opened it. 'James, I need a word, if you have time?'

James Rothsberg smiled as he placed his phone into the holder on the desk. 'Jake, I was just talking about you. Ears burning?'

'No. Not at all.'

'How's it going over at the studio? Not taxing you too much?' James leaned back in his chair and indicated for Jake to sit too. 'Pretty cool job, right?'

Jake took a seat opposite him. 'That's what I want to discuss. It's entirely inappropriate that I'm there, to be honest. I'm wasting my time, and theirs. There are less qualified people who could do the work; it's not difficult, just time-consuming. Very time-consuming.'

James gave an uncharacteristic frown. 'But it's a roster. We all do our share. It's part of your contract.'

'Yes, I know. But now I'm doing Kim's stint too.'

'So we'll rearrange it so you don't get to do it again in a hurry. Fine?'

Not fine. Jake did not want to go back there and exchange heated looks with a redheaded English rose who only had one speed: hyperdrive. He wanted to stay here and work his heart out making people better, the way he knew how. He wanted to focus on his job. This job, here, the one he'd worked so hard to get, and the one he wanted to keep. And not think about pretty little angry stomps or waste his time on non-emergencies and actresses who wanted to keep secrets. 'I'd prefer it if someone else could go.'

'And I'd prefer it if you go. I'm just off the phone with Alfredo. He's very impressed after hearing the rave review Cameron Fontaine gave you this afternoon. He's requested that you accompany them on a location shoot. To keep her happy, mainly. In fact, she's insisting on it.'

Jake felt frustration well up in his gut. 'What? A location shoot? No way. That's out of the question. What about my patients? You know, the brain-injured ones?'

His boss's palm rose. 'Jake, I'm not arguing about this. We can rearrange your schedule. It's only for a few days—mainly over the weekend, so it won't take you away from your patients here. I can give you time off in lieu. It's in the Bahamas. That should appeal, right?'

The Bahamas? What the hell…? What did that have to do with a desiccated space-odyssey landscape? The world had gone mad.

Sun. Sea. And…well, at least the fiery redhead wouldn't be there. Surely? That wasn't the kind of thing assistants did, was it? Accompany their bosses on location shoots? 'I don't know, James. I don't see how I'm the best fit for this. Send someone else.'

'You don't have any surgery booked until Tuesday. I can't see a problem,' James said, as he tapped on his laptop and looked at what Jake imagined was the OR schedule. The atmosphere became charged a little as his boss sat forward, suddenly serious. 'See, the way it works is this: the studio heads contract to the clinic. We're the best in California and everyone knows it, so they want to be associated with us. And it's very lucrative, very prestigious. My point is, Alfredo plays golf with some of the studio guys…we don't want word getting out that we renege on our contracts, do we? That our staff are unhelpful? Way too negative for us. We need you to keep them sweet.'

'When you put it like that...' It was clear this was a battle he couldn't fight. James was right, he could rearrange his outpatient clinics, he didn't have any scheduled surgery for a few days. Jake had made his feelings clear, but was big enough to accept that sometimes there were things he couldn't change.

'Plus, this kind of exposure to celebrities really helps with promoting the Bright Hope Clinic and the work Mila does there. Celebs love being involved with charities, and having our staff involved at all levels helps bring in donations. It's great leverage.'

There was a strange mist in James's eyes as he spoke of the Bright Hope Clinic. But Jake doubted whether it had as much to do with the pro bono work they were all going to do there with underprivileged kids as it had to do with the charity head, Mila Brightman. Every time James and Mila were in the same room there was a strange buzz in the air. It bordered on animosity—but there was something else there too. Fireworks, mainly.

Jake gave his friend a quick smile to show his agreement. He would not put his own needs first when kids' futures were on the line. And, yeah, he was also big enough to admit that, despite what he thought about the airhead celebrity culture, they had big hearts and deep pockets and did a lot of good…and now he was starting to go soft. 'Okay, okay, I'm packing already.'

'Great. See? Not too hard, was it? A free trip to the Bahamas? I wouldn't grumble. So, how's everything else going? How's the wonderful Cameron? Alfredo said she's had a few issues. I've heard she can be a huge pain in the—' James was interrupted by a soft tap at the door. 'Yes? Come in.'

It was Mila. As she walked in Jake saw her cheeks flush a little. She focused solely on the man in front of her. 'Hi, James. I'm so sorry to interrupt you.'

'Mila, no problem, not at all.' His boss stood immediately, suddenly looking like a lost boy rather than the accomplished professional he was. Jake hadn't been working here very long, so he didn't know what, if any, past these two had, but he smiled to himself. Whatever the hell was going on was so damned obvious to everyone—if not to them. The air had become charged in a completely different way, and Jake figured now was a good time to leave. Three was a crowd after all…

He stood to go. 'Hi, Mila. Bye, Mila. Sorry, just leaving.'

'Oh.' She whirled round, her voice a little more high-pitched than he remembered it to be. 'I didn't see you there. Hi, Jake. How's things?'

James cut in. 'Poor guy's got a difficult weekend coming up. A few days in Nassau with Cameron Fontaine.'

'Oh? Exciting.' Mila smiled, her long brown ponytail swishing as she turned her head. 'Must be hard, being you.'

'Tough job, right?' And for a split second he found himself looking forward to the break, imagining a beach at sunset, the last dying rays of sun shimmering on a mass of red curls… Damn it… He needed to get out more. What the hell was wrong with him? Thirty minutes. That's all he'd spent with Lola Bennett. Why she kept stomping into his head he didn't know. But he wished she would stop it. 'Look, I've got to get back to the studio. I'll see you two later.'

But, already lost in their own tense conversation, he doubted they'd heard him. As he ambled to the door he caught snippets, James sounding a little stilted. 'Sure, Mila, I've got the number right here.'

Mila's breathy response was, 'Great. I was just passing, and thought it'd be easier to ask in person than phone. I need a number and a quick chat about her work, character, commitment, really, whether you think she'd be a good fit for Bright Hope. But I can't stay long, I've got to meet someone in an hour.'

'Oh? Tyler?' James's voice was more of a growl at the mention of Mila's boyfriend. Jake wished he could hear this out but he didn't do gossip, no matter how tempting. And yet he still couldn't bring himself to leave just yet. He paused to fasten his bag.

Mila shook her head. 'No. It's with the cleaning company manager. We have a couple of issues with their contract.' There was a pause. 'Actually, Tyler and I split.'

'Oh? I'm sorry to hear that.' Was that interest in James's voice? No. It couldn't be. Really?

She gave a bitter laugh. 'I'm not. Now…the number for that paediatric cardiologist?'

'Yes. Right here. You don't seem too cut up about it.'

And as Jake tried to close the door without disturbing them, he heard her voice harden. 'It wasn't working, and I'd prefer not to talk about it. I don't like to get my personal life embroiled in my professional. And I'm certainly not going to discuss it with you.'

'Yes. No. Of course.' James sounded wrong-footed. Surprised by her reaction. And so was Jake, a little. Normally she was a warm-hearted woman, professional, capable and very caring. Devoted to her patients. But she did sound a little bitter right now.

And Jake really did need to go. Eavesdropping was definitely not part of his contract. Plus, he was running late for a date with a very demanding leading lady…and her very jolly English assistant.

Lola sat in the trailer, trying to focus on editing her script, but failing, badly. Usually she welcomed moments like this where she could spend some time on herself and her own work, but she was feeling restless, fidgety. Kept looking towards the door and wishing it would open.

That damned doctor. He'd been the first person to pay attention to her—to Lola Bennett—rather than her employer or her contacts, or her usefulness. Plus he'd been quite amiable in the end—once she'd set him straight on manners.

Really.

He needn't have been so nice to her. She was growing used to being in the background, which was a far cry from being a big fish in the small sea at Oxford University. But it was nothing more than she'd expected. LA was a big city after all, and everyone wanted a piece of the action.

And, well, she needed to focus on her work and the less she thought about Jake's body the better.

But it was so…so hot. Never in her wildest dreams had she thought she'd find a stroppy neurosurgeon attractive. She'd always imagined she'd get embroiled with the creative, arty type. But her cheeks burned just thinking about him.

Which was stupid.

And, besides, he'd shown no interest in her…

in *that* way. She was just a little bit lonely. And therefore vulnerable.

No. She would never be vulnerable. She was hard-working, focused and intent. Most of the time.

A knock on the door had her heart racing. 'Come in!'

'Hey, Lola Bennett.' Jake stepped into the trailer and gave her a smile. A little uncomfortable, wary maybe, but there it was. 'I've come back to check on Cameron. But I didn't see her on set and she's not here?'

'She's gone home. They're working on a different scene now—after you'd gone she did very well and they managed to catch up, but she was tired so she's gone for an early night. I called the clinic and told them she was okay and not to worry you, but you'd already set off. Don't you have your cell phone? They said they'd text you.' What was it about him that made her ramble on so much?

'I keep it on silent because it keeps ringing and disturbing me.' He dragged it from his suit jacket pocket and showed her. The strange and yet nice thing about Dr Lewis was that he wasn't the least bit affected. He was straight up. Honest. Had no pretensions or cocky swagger. And yet he was so damned hot to look at he could have been in any one of her boss's recent movies, or on the cover of a magazine. He just didn't seem to realise it. 'Oh, yes. There is a message.'

'So you've wasted your time. I'm sorry.' *Liar.* She was actually a bit pleased that he was here. Well, she would have been had her heart not started a funny little rhythm that felt like she was being kicked in the chest every few minutes. She was pleased, but judging by his frown he wasn't. 'I waited here in case you turned up. I didn't want you to think we'd all abandoned you.' The added bonus was that she could use the electricity here for free and snack on the leftover food in Cameron's refrigerator. Plus, the thought of going home to her empty, shabby apartment left her cold.

'Well, at least someone cares whether my time's wasted.' He nodded at the pile of paper on the table. 'That your script? You never got round to telling me what it's about. Please don't tell me it's another space disaster movie. I think the world has more than enough of them.'

She laughed. 'How can you say that? The

world can never have enough space desert warrior princesses. With AK47s. And very bad dialogue. Make more, I say. Lots of them. With terrible sequels.'

'No. Not sequels too. Please don't encourage them.' The irritation broken, he finally laughed, his eyes shining in the dim light of the trailer lamps. When he relaxed he was pretty damned gorgeous. 'So what kind of movies do you like, Lola?'

'Anything with a good story, really. I love characters I can identify with, with guts and emotions. I'm not big on action thrillers and definitely not horrors—unless there's a real character growth arc... Sorry, am I getting too technical? I'm doing an online course on writing screenplays and learning so much about story development. But the trouble with dissecting movies is that now I can't see one without analysing it. I'm spoilt for ever.'

'That sucks.' He picked up the front sheet of her script. 'Can I see?'

'No. Please, no.' She snatched it back, trying hard not to sound too crazy. Her screenplay was her baby and she wasn't sure it was good enough yet. 'I just don't think it's ready. My eyes only, and all that.'

'Sure, I understand.' At her wary frown he sat down on the sofa opposite. 'I'm a perfectionist too. I hate doing anything less than stellar.'

'That's why you're so good at your job.'

His eyebrows rose. 'You wouldn't know. You've hardly seen me at my best.'

'Well, you were very good with Cameron.'

'Not at first. You'd have been more impressed if you'd seen me manipulating a probe in her motor cortex…that's part of the brain…while she was still awake.' He waved his fingers in the air like a conductor and it was so out of character that she laughed.

'Believe me, I wouldn't. I wouldn't even be in the same room as you. Good God, that sounds hideous.' Although she imagined him all scrubbed up, those strong arms working on a patient. Sweat beading his furrowed brow, his gaze catching hers across a crowded operating theatre… And now she was thinking like a bad romance novel. 'Do you really do operations while your patients are still awake?'

'Sometimes it works better that way as we can

assess the patient as we go, see how they're reacting to what we're doing. It's important to make sure we're not affecting certain processes—like speech and movement. It doesn't hurt—the brain doesn't have any pain receptors.'

'*Eugh.*' Even so, how could he do that? 'I wonder if I could put that in my movie?'

'Why not? Although if it's a kids' film, you might have a few complaints. You'd have to have a rider: Do not do this at home.'

And he had a sense of humour that was refreshing. 'Surely it's not too hard? A few chopsticks and a handy pocket knife?'

'Sure, that's all there is to it. Easy. Plus fifteen years' training, one or two pesky exams. Oh, and a steady hand is a must. Otherwise…well…' He made a slicing motion at his throat.

'Hmm. Good job you have steady hands, then.' She reached out and took his hands in hers and held them straight out to see if they shook. It was just a joke. A funny little gesture, that was all. It didn't mean anything.

But the strangest thing happened when she touched him. It was like a force, a shock or a shudder shivering through her. Her stomach began to fizz in an odd way and heat spread through her, from her core to the tips of her fingers and toes.

She looked up at him to see if he'd felt the same thing and he was looking at her in a funny way. Kind of surprised, yet irritated and bemused. And his eyes were still shining, but now in a really, really good way; the blue was dark with intent and she had an urge to lean forward across the table and kiss him. Right there. As if it was the most natural thing in the world to do.

But her throat was dry and her heart was hammering, and he still had a frown and, yet, a small smile. And she couldn't kiss him. How could she kiss him? He'd think she was completely mad. And he'd be right. She was completely mad to want to kiss him. She hardly knew him. And he might not want to kiss her back.

She dragged her eyes away from his heated face and saw her script next to his arm. That was why she was here. Not for a man. Not for a kiss with a strange doctor. Who wasn't strange at all and was actually very sexy. But too distracting. She was here for her career. Just as he was. And she was a perfectionist, just like him. But he was a lot further down the track than she was. He was already hugely successful and she was just a fledgling wannabe. She had a lot of work to do.

So she let his hands go and stood up, even though her legs were wobbly, because there was something about him that made her feel off balance. 'I…er…I think I'm going to call it a day now. No doubt Cameron will be buzzing me early in the morning. It's a five a.m. call.'

'Okay. Great idea.' He stood too, and they both tried to get out of the booth at the same time and brushed against each other. His chest was hard and strong, his breath whispered over her neck, and for a few seconds she didn't know what to do. If she moved forward she'd be in his arms. Which suddenly didn't seem such a bad idea… except…it was.

He stepped back and gestured for her to go first. 'Sorry. After you.'

'Thanks.' She winced in embarrassment as she stepped out of the trailer and down the steps, wrapped her arms around her chest and started to walk towards the car lot.

He was next to her all the way. No talking. No…anything. Just walking in a strange awkward silence while her heart thump-thump-thumped and she clenched her fists tight. And she knew that nothing happening was a good thing. A very good thing. But a small part of her still clung to the fizz that bubbled in her stomach and the jerky heartbeat that made her cough a little.

When she reached her car she stopped. 'Okay, well, thanks again, Jake. I'll see you…? Actually, I'm not sure when that'll be because Cameron's going on location in a couple of days so…'

'I don't suppose you're hungry?' He'd lost that perplexed look and was back to being completely in control again. If that banquette blunder had affected him at all he didn't show it. Which made her feel as if she was going slightly mad. He gave her smile. 'I need to eat and I guess you do too. I know a great Thai place that does amazing noodles. You want to eat?'

Yes! 'No. I don't think—I…er…' *Yes. Yes. Yes. Absolutely not.*

He shook his head quite vehemently. 'I don't mean…not a date or anything. I can't do that.'

His words made her step back. 'Why? Are you married or something?' That would be a good thing. A very good thing. A very good out-ofbounds, hands-off and definitely-no-kissing kind of good thing.

But he kept on shaking his head. 'No. God, *me* married? No way. Really, no. But I'm always open to making new friends and would like some company for dinner. I can apologise again for being an idiot earlier. You can tell me about your story. Then I can show you how to manipulate chopsticks for awake brain surgery research. And you can B-I-T-C-H about your boss in safety, because I'm absolutely bound by confidentiality, and if you told me anything you'd have to kill me or sue me.'

'Oh…I wouldn't do that. Kill you, I mean. Well, not immediately. And everyone needs a friend, right?' And it was all in the name of research and nothing else, so why not? 'That's an offer I definitely can't refuse. To be honest, I'm starving. Lead on.'

So she got into her car and followed the lights of his expensive-looking sedan. Followed him from the dark studio warehouses back to the bright lights of the city, then through a maze of back streets that she knew she would never find her way out of on her own. And for the first time in a long time she felt as if things were looking up. It would be good to have a new friend in this strange but wonderful place.

If only she could stop thinking about kissing him.

CHAPTER FOUR

THE RESTAURANT WAS nothing like she'd imagined. It had basic melamine tables, white plastic chairs that she'd seen in her local two-dollar shop, and a fog of steam fragranced with seriously delicious smells of garlic and sesame oil and fish sauce.

Multicoloured paper lanterns hung from the ceiling, giving off a rosy red-orange glow, and squished in at each table were crowds of people Lola thought must be Thai nationals all chattering and laughing away in a language she didn't understand. An oddly incongruous but perfectly quirky soundtrack of heavy rock pierced the air. Who'd have imagined a place like this? It was like being back in Bangkok.

'Like it? This place is like a second home to me now,' Jake said, as he squashed in next to her at a shared table. There was no room for embarrassment here, it was a case of either sitting close or closer. And she wasn't sure if it was the cloying heat in the room or just being next to him, but she needed a cooling drink. Fast. He ran a finger down the pictures on the menu. 'I recommend the Pad Thai or the house cashew chicken. Perfection. The best Thai food on the West Coast. Fancy a beer? Wine?' He beckoned to a male server who came over, smiled and welcomed him like an old friend.

'Mr Jake. Nice to see you again. Your usual?'

'Hi, Panit, yes, please. And some...?' He looked over at Lola.

Her mouth watering, she scoured the menu for her favourite. 'Oh, yes. A beer, pork larb and a green papaya salad, please.'

Jake leaned back and looked at her, laughing. 'There was me thinking I was going to wow you with unusual flavours and yet you know more about it than me.'

'I travelled around Asia in my uni holidays... vacations. Vietnam, Laos and Thailand.' It had taken her days to convince her parents to let her take time off. They'd had jobs lined up for her, but she didn't do them. Her first strike for freedom. 'It was brilliant. Madly busy but brilliant.

And I learnt so much about the food. We even had cooking lessons over there. I came back ten pounds heavier.' She patted her hips where the noodles and rice still clung in lumps and bumps. Her dad had gone mad about that too. *You can never be too thin*, he always said.

'You look great to me.' Jake's eyes wandered to her hands, then slowly up her body until blood rushed to her cheeks just at the moment his gaze hit hers, and there it lingered for just long enough that she felt unsettled. There was something happening—and she knew it wasn't the magical lighting or the steamy atmosphere, and it certainly wasn't the beer because she hadn't had any yet—but there was definitely something scary and weird happening inside her. And if it was just happening to her then she was going to feel like an idiot if it continued.

Jake took a slug of the beer that Panit brought over and broke the connection. 'I'd love to travel more. I just haven't gotten round to anywhere that far away.'

'You've been focusing on work?'

'You bet. My plan is to get to the top of my field and then take a little time to smell the roses…

But, first, no rest for the wicked, right? You've got to push, push, push. I get the feeling you've got the same kind of drive.' Confidence oozed from him, particularly in his smile. She wondered how it would be if this were a real date rather than a non-date. How it would feel to have those hands touch her... And suddenly she wanted them on her.

Was this chemistry real?

No. It couldn't be. She shoved such fanciful ideas to the back of her mind. He'd made his intentions very clear and she was perfectly fine with that. She didn't have time in her life for anything more intimate than this sort of dinner.

The food arrived so quickly she was surprised when the server returned with steaming plates of mains and bowls of rice. Jake picked up his two chopsticks, and one of hers, and held them aloft in front of him. 'So, here we go...brain surgery one-oh-one. Basically you need one head, three probes...'

'You're not really going to...?' She squeezed her eyes half-shut and shuddered.

'And a drill...' He made a drilling sound. Then

stopped as she screwed her eyes up even tighter. 'You okay? You've gone a bit green.'

'Please. No. That is so gross.'

'And I thought you had guts, Lola Bennett.'

Did he? How? Why? 'Well, you're going to see them in a minute if you don't stop.' But she was laughing and not really grossed out at all. Although she wouldn't be queueing up to see him in action for real.

He winked. 'Another day, then. Seriously, if you decide to incorporate some medical scenes into your story I'll be happy to help with the technical details.'

'Who knows? I may just take you up on that. I do have a few medical scenes in there. Perhaps you could write them for me and I can just edit them peering from behind my fingers?'

He smiled. 'The trick, I imagine, is to just give a few spare details and not a lot of gore—unless you're writing a horror movie, in which case the more gore, the better. Everywhere.'

'Especially in the scene where it's night-time and someone hears a noise in the cellar. But no one has a torch…and they go down anyway… while we're all screaming, "No, don't do it!"'

'Aw, no? Lola, I never realised they did that— but now you mention it…every horror movie. Ever. Now you're analysing it and spoiling it for me too.' Laughing, he tucked into the food and she followed suit. It was delicious, totally authentic and quite spicy. The cold beer washed everything down well. They ate in companiable silence until he put his chopsticks down and looked at her. 'So, give me a synopsis of your story.'

'Oh. Okay. Right. Well, I've been practising my elevator pitch—basically that's for when I'm caught in an elevator with a famous director and I have two minutes to tell them about my script before they get out.'

'You get caught in elevators with directors often?'

'Not often enough. Well, never…but I'm prepared anyway in case I do. So…listen up…' No point being nervous. He wasn't going to poke fun at her. He wouldn't criticise it. He was a…friend. She tested how that felt, and it felt good. He was funny and attentive and knew great authentic places to eat and was… Did it matter whether friends were gorgeous to look at? Just looking at him was putting her off her stride, never mind about the scary fluttery thing happening inside her. 'Right… Oh, this is too hard.'

'Come on, Lola. You can do this.'

I can? He believed in her, so why didn't she?

Because so far things hadn't worked out according to her plan, and before she knew it she'd be back on the plane, the second one in her family to give up on Los Angeles hopes and dreams. And she'd have to admit the truth to her parents and she didn't want to do that until she was successful. 'Okay. Here goes: Jane Forrest is thirty, brilliant, and…dying. Her father is missing, estranged and may hold the key to her survival. How far does she need to go to find him before time runs out? How strong are the ties that bind them together after years apart, and what will it take to convince him to help?'

'Wow.' Jake nodded, not looking as if he was overly impressed. 'Great, Lola. Yeah.'

'You're not convinced?'

'Good to hear there are no outer space desert warrior princesses.' He took a mouthful of noodles. Swallowed, licked his lips and grinned. 'Sounds pretty intense.'

'It's actually very funny in parts. I'm told it's

uplifting…and sad too. I cried buckets when I wrote it and my tutor said it was one of the best scripts he'd read. It's about a woman trying to find her long-lost father, as she needs a bone-marrow transplant. Her investigation takes her all over the world to all the places he'd visited, and she learns about the great man he'd become. But she eventually comes almost full circle and finds him in the town next to where she grew up. And she gets to wondering, if he was so great, why didn't he look for her too? But also he's dying, so he can't help her. It's…I guess it's about their re-lationship, forgiveness and healing—even when healing isn't always possible.'

Elbows on the table, he steepled his fingers. 'Sounds brilliant. So why haven't you sold it yet?'

'It's not that easy—you don't just advertise on-line and get it optioned. I'm tweaking it. It needs work.'

'You need someone else to look it over…a script assessor? Your dad?' Jake's startling blue eyes lit up. 'He's been an actor and a teacher, so what's the harm?'

The harm was that no one in her family knew she was writing. There'd be too many questions—

too much she'd have to tell them. And then there'd be the letdown, the disappointment, the betrayal. And, after all that, even if her dad was still interested in reading her screenplay, what if it was rubbish? She'd never live it down. 'I don't know. It's like…it's like handing over your heart and giving someone carte blanche to stomp over it.'

'Stomping runs in the family?'

'We're champion stompers actually. Won awards for it… We are stomping elite.'

'But he wouldn't do that. Surely not?' Jake studied her for a moment. His eyes really were stunning and she didn't want to stop looking at them. Her stomach felt a swooping sensation every time their gazes connected. Knowing she was on a highway to nowhere, she looked away as he spoke. 'You miss them?'

'Of course, every day.' So much. But she had to strike out on her own. She was going to be a success on her terms, then she would go home and celebrate with them. If they were still speaking to her. She turned back to him, wanting to put the focus on him for a while. 'Don't you miss your family too? Where are they? Didn't you say they were north somewhere?'

'Van Nuys. Just parents. I'm an only child.'

'Not far at all, then. Do you see them a lot?'

'They'd probably say not enough, but...you know how it is.' He shrugged, a little closed suddenly, and she wondered why.

'You're busy living your life, right?'

'Sounds selfish when you put it like that.' Eyebrows rising, he huffed out a breath. 'Which is a huge guilt trip for me, seeing as they fought hard for me to do that. Too damned hard at times.' Then he looked away and breathed out heavily.

She felt as if she'd put a big dollop of down on the conversation and thought briefly about putting her hand on his shoulder to show him solidarity, but thought better of it. She couldn't work out why she had this sudden urge to touch the man. Or to make him feel better. 'Go and see them, then.'

He turned back to her. 'That easy, right?'

'Look, I don't know the circumstances, but I'd say some communication is better than none.' She was giving family relationship advice? Go figure.

He finished his beer and stared at the empty glass, clearly not wanting to elaborate. Then he turned to her and smiled. 'You know what? I just might go up there and see them—although I'm going to Nassau this weekend.'

'You too, eh? Lucky duck. I'll be stuck here with the pooches. Cameron has three dogs she adores. And I don't particularly. They're very spoilt,' she finished in a whisper. She would have to play mama while everyone else swanned off to the Bahamas. She refused to allow images of Jake sunbathing into her head. But they came and hung around for a few moments anyway, making her blush. It seemed her mind was in conflict over Jake Lewis. On the one hand, it understood and respected the whole friends thing…and on the other it wanted sneaky, semi-naked thoughts. Actually, it wanted full-blown, butt-naked thoughts. Clearly she was going mad. It was time for bed. Alone. 'Actually, talking of work…it's getting late, I really should be getting home.'

He glanced at his watch and nodded. 'I suppose so.'

He got the bill and refused to discuss her paying a share. Which was another big fat tick for the doctor—because even though she tried to pay it was nice to have someone looking out for her for a change. 'I'll get it next time,' she promised.

'Next time?' There was a smile in his voice and a question. As they walked towards her car she wondered what to do or say now. Would there be a next time? Had she said something inappropriate? Should she kiss him on his cheek, both cheeks, shake hands? Or just walk away? 'Next time sounds good, Lola. It'll have to be after Nassau, though. But, before you go, I have something to ask you…'

'Oh? Yes?' Her voice rose a little as her heart began to hammer.

'Strange question, I know, but is Cameron seeing anyone at the moment?'

Oh, God. Her stomach tumbled. *Here we go again.* Stupid. Stupid. She'd read the signs all wrong. He wasn't remotely interested in her, he was interested in Cameron. She should have known. History repeating itself over and over. That was why he'd insisted it wasn't a date. Stupid fool. When would she learn? No one was interested in her. Plenty of interest in her boss, though.

Hoping he hadn't heard the pathetic *hope* in her voice, she tried to keep her answer in friend territory. 'Not at the moment. That I'm aware of. She was dating Marc Jason a few months ago but that fizzled. It's always the same—busy sched-ules that never coincide and no one wanting to put their relationships first, because that's the kiss of death to a career-minded person.' And, okay, she was just adding that last bit on to remind him that he was a career-minded person too, and that a relationship with Cameron would never work. It was for his own good. Plus, putting a negative spin on it made her feel a teensy bit better.

'Oh. Okay.' He frowned again, as if he was thinking about something serious—weirdly, he didn't have that dog panting tongue thing going on like most of Cameron's admirers. Maybe he was working out a strategy for when they were in Nassau. A sensible and driven man was Jake, and very goal oriented. Maybe bedding an A-list actress was on that list of goals. Along with shaming the personal assistant. Well, he could tick that one off his list already.

'Do you want me to put a word in for you? Is that what this is all about? Is that what dinner was about? The non-date? You're interested in Cam-eron because, let's face it, why wouldn't you be? So you thought you'd pay for dinner and buy her secrets from me? Or worse—if you can't have her, you'd try to have me as consolation prize? Second best, right? Here we go again.' Fighting back bitter tears, Lola stomped—yes, she stomped perfectly—towards her car.

But Jake caught her up and pulled her to a complete halt. 'What...? You think...? Me? With Cameron? Are you for real?'

'It wouldn't be the first time that has happened to me.'

'Hell, no. You've totally got this upside down. Not at all. Not at all. I was asking...' again the serious frown and a pause '...to see who would be on the private plane, who to expect generally. How many people I have to look after.' He gave an embarrassed wince because clearly he wasn't convincing anyone with that line. 'But really? Has that happened before? A guy has taken you out so you could introduce him to Cameron?'

'Yep. One too many times.' Lola closed her eyes briefly at the memory, the sharp sting of betrayal. How gullible she'd been...and was continuing to be. Would she never learn? 'But she is very beautiful and rich and famous and on another level. Why wouldn't anyone be attracted to her?'

Conversely, then, why would anyone be interested in her?

Jake's jaw stiffened, his eyes blazing in the streetlight, his grip on her arm firm. 'I am not attracted to Cameron Fontaine.'

'Then you must be blind.'

Strangely, out of nowhere a smile formed on his lips. 'Oh, no, my vision is perfect.'

'Then you must be gay.' *Please, for the love of all women, including Cameron Fontaine if absolutely necessary, do not be gay.*

'No way.' He stepped closer, so she could see his chest rising and falling, could feel the warmth of his breath on her skin. Could smell the most exquisite scent of man and medicine and spice.

'Then what…?'

'Then this.' And he was suddenly too close. Not close enough. He pulled her to face him and his fingertips lifted her chin. '*This*, Lola.'

His mouth pressed against hers, gently at first, and her body responded in a flush of heat that pooled deep in her core. Every part of her craved him, craved to touch him, to kiss him, to feel him against her.

Initial instinct told her that she shouldn't kiss

him back, but something deeper, something intense had her opening her mouth and tasting him. And he tasted good. So good. She felt as inquisitive as the doomed teenagers stepping into the dark basement, and as filled with adrenalin. Knowing, like them, she was headed to disaster but doing it anyway.

She wound her arms around his neck and pulled him closer as his tongue slid past her lips, stoking the furnace that had lit inside her. She moaned at the pleasure of him filling her mouth, of the curling clench in her gut, at the sensations that ran up and down her spine, just being in his arms.

Leaning her against her car door, his hands cupped her face and he pressed harder against her, kissing her open-mouthed, and wet and hungry. She could feel how much he wanted her. How much he wanted something from her.

And like listening to an old-fashioned vinyl record scratching to a stop, she felt a visceral catch as her body stiffened. She put her hands on his chest and pushed a little away from him. 'Stop. No. This...this isn't...'

'What is it? What's wrong?' But he didn't let

her go as he hauled in deep ragged breaths, kissed the top of her head and stayed close.

'I can't stop thinking about Cameron and there are too many questions racing in my head. Too many reasons not to do this. Please, I think you should just go.'

'Lola, believe me, this is not about Cameron. She is the furthest thing from my mind. I don't want to go. I want to stay right here, doing this.'

Damn it. Jake's hands dropped from her face as he struggled to control his breathing. God, she was hot. He couldn't describe the way he felt with her pressing against him, kissing him. The fun she found in her life despite everything, the positive spin, the humility. She was a bundle of energy that he wanted to capture, to slow down, to have in his bed. And he'd blown it by saying the wrong thing at the wrong time. Each time he thought he knew what he was doing, things took a very unexpected turn.

Error number one: inviting Lola out for dinner in the first place, when he should have gone home and packed for the break he clearly needed. Because, no matter what he might have said about it being a non-date, the words and the reality were on two very opposing sides.

Error number two: mentioning Cameron at such a defining moment. He'd been thinking about trying to convince Lola's boss to seek medical help, and had wondered whether he should suggest Cameron confide in the baby's father too. He couldn't tell Lola that Cameron was pregnant. That would betray a professional confidence and was something he would never do.

But he did want to keep kissing Lola. 'I was stupid to mention her. I'm sorry I've ruined the moment.'

'I'm sorry? So you can actually say it? Now, there's a revelation.' Lola gazed up at him and he could see the hesitation and the desire still there, and that she was fighting it. Resigned to it being over. 'It was already heading in the wrong direction, right? It wasn't a date, you said openly that you didn't want that, and things have just gotten a little out of control.'

He huffed out a long breath. 'I wanted to kiss you.'

'And I wanted to kiss you back.' She gave him a small smile that was at once coy and sexy.

That gave him some hope, as he wasn't finished with the kissing. Although everything she was saying made absolute sense, his body had other things on its mind. 'So we could have a re-run?'

The red hair swung as she shook her head. 'No, Jake. It was an itch that we had to scratch. But it's done now and I don't think we should do it again. I get the feeling we want very different things.'

'I don't know what I want, Lola. At least I did yesterday. I did this morning. Now I'm not sure, but I think it definitely involves you and a lot more kissing.'

'See? Now I'm messing things up for you.' She turned away from him and unlocked her car. Climbed in. Wound down the window. All in the quick-paced way that she did everything. 'I think it'd be a good idea if I'm not around when you come over to see Cameron. Don't worry, I'll make myself scarce.'

Then she gunned the engine and was gone.

She was right. Kissing was messing with his head. A few days on location with a demanding celebrity would see him back to his normal self— one who didn't do random kissing in the street with a woman he'd only just met.

Although he had a feeling that getting back to normal might take a little time, and that a certain Lola Bennett would be stomping through his dreams tonight.

CHAPTER FIVE

JAKE HAD TO admit that flying by private jet was going to be pretty damned cool. He wasn't easily impressed, but he was looking forward to this part of the potentially mind-numbing trip more than anything else. Somehow he'd managed to score a flight with Cameron, and he needed to find time to talk to her about his suspicions of her pregnancy and what antenatal care she should be having.

Thankfully he could concentrate on that, and then try to get some shut-eye after failing to get a decent night's sleep for the first time in his life. Medical school then interning—being woken up at any time of day and night and expected to respond immediately with both a ready smile and a correct diagnosis—had taught him to be able to sleep anywhere he needed, any time. He could power up and down on demand as easily as his trusty laptop.

Except for the last few nights—when he hadn't been able to get the taste and smell of Lola, along with memories of her easy laugh and mesmerising smile, out of his head. All the more reason he needed this break—mind-numbing or not—to reaffirm his work focus and equilibrium. He would approach it as he did everything else, with single-minded determination to do it to the highest standard.

It was, after all, what he'd promised his father he would do—and the only thought going through his brain right now, other than Lola, were the words he'd used at his father's bedside in the hospital. *'I'll pay you back, double, triple what you've given me. Just get well and come home.'* His dad had paid too high a price for Jake to lose focus.

After ditching his car at valet parking, he strode into the private airfield departure lounge, which was more like a converted hangar than anything particularly luxurious, and was immediately greeted by a cacophony of shouts, hysterical screaming and wild yapping.

'Get her, quick, grab her, hurry!' Cameron was screaming, as a small brown dog wearing a studded diamanté collar, head down and teeth bared, scampered faster than Jake imagined a dog that size could go towards an open door that led to the tarmac. Dropping his bags, Jake set off in hot pursuit, dodging air crew, ground crew, piles of luggage, a refuelling lorry and, thankfully, but only just, a catering trolley heading straight for him.

The dog, seemingly enjoying this game of one hundred metre dash, bounded towards the steps of a private Cessna.

'Peanut! Sit. Sit!' From behind Jake a stern but breathless English voice bellowed through the hangar and, unbelievably, the dog came to an abrupt halt at the foot of the steps. 'Naughty girl! Now, come here.'

Lola?

Jake took the opportunity to creep forward and grab the dazed puppy, securing it under his arm. *I did not sign up for this.*

Then he turned to see the cause of his insomnia, who was doubled over, trying to haul in air while simultaneously juggling two other bejewelled, yapping dogs close to her breasts. *Lucky damned pooches.*

And there he was again—losing himself.

It hadn't occurred to him that she'd be here, but maybe she'd come to wave the Nassau-bound party off? Making sure her boss actually left the ground? Not such a bad idea. Shame she'd be stuck with those dogs, though. Nightmare. 'Peanut? That's a name? I thought it was something you had with beer.'

'Sorry, it's chaos as always. Can we do a swap? Please take Butter for a second while I secure Peanut. Yes, we have Peanut, Butter and this is Jelly. I know.' Lola straightened up, offered one of the other dogs to Jake. He couldn't tell whether she was glaring at him or the dogs. Either way there was no smile, and he felt guilty by association. 'Not my choices, by the way. So, Peanut is the devil incarnate—you need to keep a special eye on her or she'll be AWOL in five seconds flat. Butter is the glutton and Jelly is the sweetie. Take my advice, never, ever get three puppies at the same time.'

'It never crossed my mind to get even one. Ever.' He swapped one wriggling jiggling dog for another, which leaned in close and sniffed his face. Its breath smelt like rank dog biscuits and its claws were sharp. Then it stuck out its pink tongue. For a second he thought it was going to take a bite, but instead it began to lick his cheek with unhindered gusto. 'Ugh. No. Er… Butter. Stop.'

He held it at arm's length, looked over at Lola, who was now grinning at his discomfort, and then wished he hadn't as he noticed the smooth curve of her mouth and her clipped-back hair, the soft cotton flowered top and loose skirt that blew a little round her legs in the light wind. That flight couldn't come soon enough.

With a rise of her eyebrows Lola nodded. 'She likes you. That's her way of kissing.'

'Yuck. Personally, I prefer the human way.' The words tumbled out of his mouth before he could stop them, and the memories of the other night tumbled too, making him feel hot and unsatisfied all over again. It was obvious that Lola was thinking the same, as she bit down on her bottom lip and looked away red-cheeked, leaving him wondering exactly where things would have ended up if he hadn't uttered those kiss-of-death—or rather, death-of-kiss—words: *Cameron Fontaine.*

'Yes. Well…' Lola attached a lead to Peanut's collar, took Butter from his outstretched hands and put all three dogs on the ground. 'Unfortunately she hasn't mastered the art of tact yet.'

'Like her owner.' *And me.* Jake threw Lola a smile, not sure if it was reassuring or what the hell it was. He didn't know the required etiquette for talking to someone who really didn't want to share the same air as him, and had told him as much.

Lola looked up at him through dark, thick eyelashes, solemn and serious. 'Er…about the other day—'

'No need…really.'

'It's just, you know, bad timing.'

'It's fine, I understand.' Although he didn't. Seriously, he was a surgeon, dealing with science and facts and black and white. All this chaos and acting and kissing was way beyond his comprehension.

But he did understand her reluctance to want to do it again. She'd been taking up far too much of his head space. He preferred his liaisons to be brief, satisfactory and forgettable. That way he could focus entirely on his work and paying back his dad. Just the thought of the debt he owed gave Jake a jolt in his chest.

'Lola! Do hurry up! And you too, Dr Lewis.' Ms Fontaine was waving and indicating that it was time to leave. 'Don't make us late. Lola, where are your bags?'

'Sorry! Coming!' Lola started towards her boss, encouraging the three yapping stooges to follow on their leads. 'Come on, sweeties. Hurry up. This way.'

But Jake held back, suddenly off balance all over again. 'What? Your bags?'

'Oh. Yes.' Lola threw the comment over her shoulder, like scraps to a hungry bird. 'Apparently Mommy doesn't want to leave her babies—for some reason she's come over more broody than usual and can't bear to be parted from them. So we're all coming too. Normally I would be thrilled at the idea of going to Nassau for the weekend, but—'

He never got to hear the *but,* although he imagined what it was, as the jet engines powered into life, the noise sending thoughts and words into the wind, and that much of the *but* had to do with him and that kiss. Or maybe he was reading too much into it. Though the blush on Lola's cheeks wasn't due to make-up, and the tone in her voice hadn't been wistful and hopeful. It had been as wary as he felt, a warning almost.

Out on the tarmac a fierce draught blew Lola's red curls round her face, and the dogs' mouths opened and closed with apparent indignation at the racket, but Jake couldn't hear anything over the engine din. He was beginning to realise that whatever plans he'd made were about to crash into oblivion. He was not going to get private time to discuss Cameron's pregnancy. The attraction to her assistant was not abating any time soon. And a decent night's sleep was clearly going to become a thing of the past.

In truth, Lola coming on this trip was the worst possible outcome he could imagine.

Cameron had fallen asleep in one of the sumptuous red and cream leather sofas on board, and Jake was doing a good impression of the same thing. However, as he'd been seated next to her, Lola could see that even though his eyes were closed, his breathing wasn't rhythmic and slow. He was just pretending to be asleep.

He was pretending? Just so he didn't have to talk to her? Charming.

And the problem was, even on a plane like this where seating was plentiful and generous, he was still too close for any kind of comfort. Worse, that ridiculous urge to reach out and touch him hovered around—to just lay her hand against his chest or his arm, or something. The other night had been a close-run thing, and she'd felt mortified when Cameron had demanded she accompany them on this trip when she'd have far preferred not to see Jake again. Somehow she would have to keep her distance. The man was no good for her plans.

After five and a half uncomfortable hours of dark silence, followed by awkward conversation whilst trying to contain three excitable puppies, they landed in Nassau. So much for private flying—not one sip of champagne had passed her lips; Miss Fontaine was on a *clean* diet so that meant everyone else was too.

The lunch had been delicious, though—a decent serving of fresh raw taco shells with spicy vegetables, salsa and cashew cheese. Slightly strange, but far better than any economy class, ever, even if just for the real knives and forks instead of plastic ones, and real linen napkins.

'Well, that was very acceptable. I think I'm spoiled for flying ever again,' she whispered to Jake, just for something to say as they stood shoulder to shoulder at the top of the steps, waiting to disembark. Cameron had insisted on going first, making a grand entrance for the waiting local paparazzi, while the staff hung around in her slipstream. 'I don't suppose you could convince the boss that drinking buckets and buckets of French champagne is very good for you? She's got it into her head that alcohol is very bad, but I'd love a glass.'

He shook his head and frowned. 'A cold beer would have been great, but…not for Cameron. She shouldn't be drinking.'

'Why not?'

He looked pensive. 'Er…I suppose she has to maintain her figure for continuity reasons for the film. No alcohol for the foreseeable future.'

'Spoilsport. I thought you might be on my side.' But, then, she supposed, she'd pushed him away the other day so why should he do anything to please her? 'Here goes. Down the steps… Now, don't say anything as you walk by the cameras, just keep looking ahead. Oh, and could you take one of these, please? Peanut's very wriggly again. I don't think she likes flying.'

'She's definitely not one for cattle class, that's for sure.' Jake didn't look enamoured about carrying a Chihuahua, and she had to admit that a beautiful, tall, toned man carrying a tiny dog did look funny. But he took it anyway, in one hand, and with the other he steadied her down the steps, a gentle touch on her elbow. For a second Lola felt as if she were the star, but the thrumming of her heart and the hot flush to her cheeks just highlighted the shy teenager inside her. Sometimes she didn't know how Cameron dredged up all that confidence every day, every hour. It was exhausting.

The limo journey from the airport, under a cloudless bright blue sky, took them west past candy-coloured high-rise apartments and along palm-tree-lined roads, through a maze of canals towards Old Fort Bay and the many private residences dotted along the coastline. Beyond the fancy gates and majestic buildings Lola got a glimpse of white sandy beaches and a turquoise sea. Only the rich and famous bought homes here.

One day, she thought.

Wait… Oh, wow. Actually, today… The car turned right into a long gravel driveway, meandered through lush, verdant bushes and eventually came to a stop outside a large white colonial villa clothed in bright pink creeping bougainvillea. 'Oh, my God. It's gorgeous.'

Stunned, Lola bundled the dogs out of the car and gave instructions to the driver as Cameron disappeared into the house. This was way beyond anything she'd imagined.

'I wasn't expecting this. I thought we'd be at a resort or something with the others.' Jake looked equally impressed as he carried luggage from the car boot to the door. He peered up at the magnificent building, then at the manicured front lawn and frowned. 'Before we go in, Lola, can I ask you something?'

Uh-oh. If it was about the other night she'd just about die.

If it was about kissing again she would do that first, and then just about die. 'Sure. What is it?' It was as nonchalant as she could get, in between palpitations.

He pointed to the house. 'What the hell has this all got to do with a space warrior odyssey?'

She breathed out, a flicker of disappointment subsumed by good old common sense. Then she laughed, because she was a damned fool to even think… He wasn't the kind of guy to try again after rejection. 'Oh. Well, it's a flashback scene or a dream sequence, going back to pre-apocalyptic Earth, or something. But between you and me I think it's just a good excuse for a jolly.'

He gave her a funny look. 'A jolly what?'

'A jolly. It means…it means a work thing that's really just all about play.'

'You Brits say the strangest things.' But he was laughing and for a moment the air between them seemed less strained. Maybe, if they kept their conversations superficial, and maintained a decent distance, they could reach some sort of friendly equilibrium after all. Maybe he could be in one wing and she'd isolate herself in the opposite one. The place was certainly big enough. Yes, distance was the solution.

A young woman appeared at the door and explained in a melodic Bahamian accent that she was Tina, the housekeeper, and to please leave everything to her. 'Miss Fontaine has requested sole use of the house. I have put you and the… Dr

Jake...' The woman peered up at Jake and smiled. For a moment Lola thought the housekeeper was going to curtsy or kiss him, or just old-fashioned swoon. 'Good afternoon, Dr Jake. Welcome to The Haven. I hope you'll be happy here.'

He shook her outstretched hand. 'I'm sure I will. Thank you, Tina.'

'Anything you want, just go right ahead and ask,' Tina sighed.

Lola sighed too, but hers was more through irritation. *That's right, lady, keep right on looking. I've kissed that mouth.*

A strange and breath-sapping spike of something lodged underneath Lola's ribcage. Must have been the raw taco shells not agreeing with her, she decided, and nothing at all to do with a fierce possessive streak that scuttled through her. Jake was not her property and she would not be jealous of women looking at him like that. Yes, he was gorgeous. Yes, he was dashing and charming. So what? No big deal.

She'd switched off momentarily and hadn't heard what the housekeeper had been saying, but as she tapped behind her across the marble floors through the palatial house, then out past a huge infinity pool, Lola realised that they were being taken to a different building.

'In here, please, Miss Bennett.' They'd stopped outside a smaller, single-storey villa, cream and white with another deep red bush growing up the side, a small picket-fenced garden and a wrought-iron outside table for two on a deck overlooking the ocean. It was more private and secluded than the grand villa. It was, in fact, like a cosy honeymoon retreat.

No. No flipping way. Blood rushed to her cheeks. She couldn't…wouldn't…shouldn't be here with him. She should be in the big house, tending to her boss's every need. Even that was preferable to being in a honeymoon hideaway with Jake. 'I…er…there's been a mistake…'

'No. No mistake.' Oblivious to Lola's growing panic, the housekeeper was still chattering away. 'The Lodge is for you and the doctor to share at Miss Fontaine's insistence. Two bedrooms, two bathrooms. There are interconnecting phones to the main house in the kitchen, the lounge and each bedroom. But Miss Fontaine said, please, to let her rest for a few hours. She will call if she needs anything.'

'Okay.' Lola blew out a big breath. This was so not what she'd had in mind for superficial and distant. But if there was one thing she knew about her boss it was that she wouldn't change her mind once it was made up. She and Jake would be sharing. Period. 'Well, first, I need to get the dogs some water and some shade. It's too hot for them. I could take them for a walk around the grounds. I saw a lovely little shaded area they could play in back near the big house.' Anything to distract her from the fact that she would be sharing living quarters with a god.

Tina smiled as she bent to give the dogs a stroke. 'Aren't they adorable? The beach out front is private, so they can run around there under the trees. I have a little dog of my own over in the staff annexe, they can come play any time. I can take them now, give you a break?'

'Thanks, but the walk will do us good after being cooped up on a plane.' Truthfully, it was just an excuse for some Jake-free time.

But the traitorous puppies pattered quietly into the cool lodge, obviously exhausted from their first-class travelling ordeal, found a plump cushion each on a white rattan sofa and fell asleep.

The housekeeper fussed around the light, bright house, showing them the modern kitchen facilities, the menu—because, yes, The Haven had its own chef—and the well-stocked pantry and fridge. Then she left, leaving them to decide who had which bedroom, and what the hell to do next.

And then there were two.

Lola glanced over at Jake, who was staring at the beach out of a huge picture window in the lounge. 'Er…how shall I put this? Do you want to have a look at the bedrooms and decide where you want to sleep?'

Eyebrows rising, Jake grinned. 'Now you're talking.'

'I didn't mean… No. I meant—'

'I was joking, Lola. Don't look so worried. Take whichever room you want and I'll have the other.' He bent and unzipped his bag, grabbed something from it. 'I'm going for a swim while I have the chance. Coming?'

She imagined him in board shorts. A naked chest. Bare skin. Soaking wet. And swallowed through a dry throat. 'Er… No. I don't want to leave these little guys on their own and I really

do need to unpack. And Cameron might call…
and I'm thirsty…' And…she was rambling again.

'Hey.' He stepped closer. 'Don't worry, Lola.
It's all under control. How about I have a swim,
then take over childcare while you go and cool
off? A roster system?'

'Oh, okay, that sounds great. Thanks. It is very
hot. And I could do with a swim. Later, when you
get back.'

The smile slipped. 'Sure. And that way we need
never be in the same room for longer than a few
moments. Just at cross-over. That's what you
want? Right?'

Her heart began to hammer—he was very
forthright when he wanted to be. Direct and to
the point. She supposed he had to be in his line of
work—couldn't pussy-foot around a bad diagnosis. But it left her feeling exposed and vulnerable.
She wasn't used to people speaking their minds
quite so openly. Besides, she didn't know what
she wanted in relation to their living arrange-
ments. 'I just think…in light of the other night…it
would be better if our paths didn't cross so much.'

'Understood.' He took a step away, then turned.
'It was only a kiss, Lola. We can move on.'

'Of course. Yes! Only a kiss! I've already moved on. No problem!' As if she kissed people she'd just met all the time.

Only a kiss, yes. But a very nice one at that. And she didn't kiss strangers. Ever. She didn't kiss random men. She didn't kiss men she thought were just okay. She kissed men she liked. And she liked Jake. That was a massive part of the problem. She liked him. Too much, it seemed. 'You'd better go get changed then.'

While she wandered into the open-plan kitchen, he disappeared into a bathroom, returning moments later with a white towel looped round his shoulders, beach shorts slung low over slender hips. She tried very hard not to look, she really did, but she couldn't help it. He was there, walking across the room, larger than life. Her gaze travelled upwards from his hips, past a smattering of dark hair, tanned washboard abs, a broad chest, to a smirking mouth.

For a few seconds she remembered the taste of him. The heat. And she clung to the kitchen countertop as the same heat shimmered through her. How the hell would she be able to stay here with that kind of reaction going on?

And when her eyes settled on his she knew that it was going to be almost impossible. There was humour there in his eyes, and teasing, and it fired an unwanted need in her core.

She dragged her eyes away, found a voice, albeit fractured. 'Enjoy.'

'You look like you just did.' He winked. 'See you later.'

CHAPTER SIX

LOLA WAS PROUD of herself. She'd managed to spend the rest of the day in avoidance mode. Had eaten dinner with Jake and Cameron, which had passed pleasantly enough with small talk and chit-chat about movies and brain surgery—although, Lola noticed, he hadn't offered to show Cameron how to do wide-awake surgery with chopsticks, and he was just a little more reserved around the actress.

Then Lola had taken the dogs for a late-night walk on her own, and had returned to find a quiet lodge. Jake had gone to bed and there'd been no further awkward conversation. She'd fallen asleep after only a couple of hours lying in bed wondering what the hell tomorrow would bring.

And thinking about his mouth. That body. That smile.

In the next damned room.

And how she was going to survive being stuck in close proximity to him?

After her morning puppy walk she returned to find the interconnecting phone ringing and no Jake in sight. Thank God. 'Hello!'

'Lola, honey, it's me.'

'Hi, Cameron! Beautiful day.'

'Sure is. Listen, Alfredo wants to take me on a boat trip to one of the private islands this morning, meet some of his friends. Take care of the babies, will you? They wouldn't be safe on a boat. I'll be back after lunch, then we can all go to the set.'

'Of course. Have fun. See you later.'

'Was that Cameron?' Jake's voice behind her made her heart bounce to a jerky beat.

She steadied it before turning to find him dressed in workout gear and slightly out of breath. After yesterday's staring faux pas she'd promised herself not to look too closely, so settled on trying to get the swanky coffee machine to work. She fiddled with the little shiny plastic capsules, chose a silver one, popped it in. 'Coffee?'

'Yes, thanks.'

'Been for a run?'

'Working out. There's a gym in the basement up at the house. I thought I might see Cameron there, but she didn't appear. What's the plan?' He wandered to the cabinet, pulled out a cup. Back in her line of vision. He looked sweaty, arm muscles pumped. Hair dishevelled. All kinds of hot. *No. Not looking.*

'Cameron probably worked out last night—she prefers to do it in the evenings. She's going out, back around noon, then we're to accompany her to the set.'

Jake was staring at her with a strange look on his face, which he wiped as soon as he realised she was watching him. 'So we have a free morning?'

'Just Cameron-free. Three hours or so.' Lola added skimmed milk to her coffee and started making his. Trying not to make eye contact. It felt as if she'd said something wrong, but couldn't put her finger on anything relevant. Or maybe it was just the kiss hovering between them again. She needed to get out. 'I have a ton of stuff to do. Actually, I'll go and make a start.'

His hand on her wrist stopped her, his heat

seeping into her skin and through her body. 'You haven't had your coffee, Lola.'

'Thanks. No. Well…I can take it with…' She couldn't take her eyes off his hand, long fingers, neat nails. Skilled and powerful, whether holding chopsticks, a scalpel or probes. Hands that had cupped her face so intensely.

Yes, that kiss was definitely there, the huge elephant in the room. She swallowed deeply.

He looked down and hurriedly drew his hand away from her wrist. And she wanted to grab his hand and put it right back, but he pulled out some croissants from the bread bin. 'I'm never going to survive on a skinny actress's rabbit food. I asked the chef to get something decent for us to eat. You want some? I won't tell anyone, it'll be our secret?'

'No, thanks.'

He watched her. 'You don't like them or don't want them? Two different things.'

'I'm trying to be healthy. There's some fruit in the fridge, I'll have that.' There was also champagne, she'd noted, and wondered if he'd requested that too. She watched as flaky crumbs dropped from his lip onto the plate and her stomach rumbled. God, she wanted a bite. And not just of the croissant.

As if he could read her mind, he held it out to her. 'Believe me, if you eat with Cameron every day you'll be more than healthy but not very happy. Or full. And definitely not satisfied. Besides, the brain is made up of sixty per cent fat—we need it to think, work, be. So come on, just a mouthful. This is delicious. All that butter. So good.' He bent and rummaged in the bread bin again, pulled out another pastry. 'Oh, look, here's one with chocolate. Chocolate for breakfast—sinful. In the Bahamas…in the sunshine. Just a small piece. Come on…I promise not to tell a soul.'

'Oh, go on, then, just a little bit. I have zero will-power.' She laughed, taking the *pain au chocolat* and tearing off a piece, which she unashamedly popped into her mouth. It was indeed delicious. 'So you're being my enabler now? The chocolate is the gateway drug, then the croissant is the road to hell.'

He dipped his head to look her directly in the eyes. 'I'm just trying to be friendly. The way I see it, we have to get along here. We have a small house and we're going to be spending a lot of time together. Either we try to put the kiss behind us and make a fresh start, or one of us will have to explain to Cameron our predicament and ask to bunk in with her. I can't see that going down well. But I can't live with tension and awkwardness here either.'

Again the direct approach. It was confronting, but also refreshing. She studied him for a moment. Those dark blue eyes weren't playing her, but actually genuinely trying to reach a solution. She could do this. 'Okay. Fresh start.'

'Great. Eat. Good?'

Was it rude to tear it apart with her teeth? 'Oh, God, yes. Brain food? Just think how much more clever I'll be after eating it.'

'I didn't say it would make you more clever. But what the hell…if it makes you eat, genius. Now, if only I had something to drink too…'

'Oh, your coffee…I forgot.' She put the pastry down for a moment while she found him a purple plastic capsule and set the machine. In a few moments the sounds of gurgling filled the silence.

Once he'd finished eating he gave her a satisfied smile. 'I was just talking to Tina up at the house. She says there's some excellent snorkelling over

near Lyford Cay. If we had time we could char-
ter a boat and go further offshore, but we only
have a couple hours—there's still some interesting fish just off the beach. You fancy heading
off and having a look? We can take a couple of
motor scooters.'

'What? Now?' Up close and personal with a
semi-naked Jake? No way. Once was bad enough.
Or, rather, good enough. Too good. That wasn't
her idea of a fresh start. 'What about Cameron?'

'Well, we're here to work, but we can't work if
the boss isn't around, now, can we?' He shook his
head. 'Have you ever snorkelled in the Bahamas
before? Ridden a motor scooter?'

Sharing a standing-up breakfast was one thing,
sharing a half-naked adventure was something
altogether different. 'Snorkelling? Motor scooters? My job isn't the same as yours, Jake, waiting around until someone gets sick. I have other
things to do. Lots of things.'

'Can they wait?'

'Says the self-confessed workaholic.'

'Yes, I am… But Tina said if we do nothing else
while we're here we must do some snorkelling.
She has all the gear. And I'm hardly extending

my surgical skills sitting around here, am I? What will I do…? Practise my injection technique on an orange?'

He picked up an orange from the fruit bowl and threw it into the air and caught it. Then picked up another and juggled the two. Then three. His arms flexed as he threw and caught in effortless yet hypnotising fluid movements. She could see his back muscles tighten and release, his shoulders working, the wry smile as he concentrated, almost meditative. God, he was…well, her gut prickled with heat. She became acutely aware that there was just the two of them here. That kiss may have been put aside, but the way it made it her feel hadn't been. Her fingers shook as she started to fill the dishwasher just to do something other than watch him. He caught the oranges in one hand and smiled again.

'You did that?' Her voice was thick with need. She coughed, tried not to think about his body, lowered her voice an octave. 'You injected oranges?'

'Yes, to get the angle right. And practised my suturing on pigskin…then on humans…my classmates, myself…' He put the oranges back, serious again. 'Okay, you're right. I hear you on the work issue. I have to catch up on some reading and there's research I'm assisting with…'

For just a few minutes he'd been carefree and fun, and she didn't want to lose that Jake to a serious Jake. But how could she go with him when she felt like this? 'It sounds lovely…maybe another time. Tomorrow, if we get a chance. There's a list of errands I need to do today. I can't take off and play. Besides, we have the dogs to think about.'

'Tina could have the dogs. I could help you with the errands when we get back.'

Lola lifted her smartphone from the countertop and scrolled through her task list. 'Because finding a decent manicurist on Nassau who can drop everything and come over as Cameron requires is the kind of thing you do every day.'

'Whoa. I didn't realise it would be that kind of difficult.' He looked horrified, eyes wide and panicked. 'That sounds way out of my comfort zone. Give me something easier to do, I don't know… negotiate world peace? But first snorkel?'

What could she say? *I'd like to, but if there was*

*ever a possibility of drowning in lust I'd be vic-
tim number one.* 'I just...'

'You just what?' He was scrutinising her face,
his jaw taut, eyes narrowed. Then his whole body
stilled. 'Ah. I get it, now. You just...don't want to
snorkel with *me*, that right? Sorry I took so long
to catch on.' Grabbing his half-finished coffee, he
started to walk outside to the deck and the mood
turned decidedly dark. 'I hear ya, loud and clear,
Lola. I won't bother you again.'

He'd gone way past serious Jake and was somewhere on the edge of angry Jake. She followed
him outside, feeling hollowed out. 'Jake, I do want
to go snorkelling. It sounds fun. I'll come. I was
trying to be dedicated to my work... You of all
people know how that is.' Did he believe her?

'Yeah, I do. But, you know, for one second there
I thought, Let's stuff work for a while. But don't
worry, I'll go on my own.'

'No. No, I'll come. I want to, really. I'm sorry.
Please.'

He looked at her, weighing up her words. She
wasn't sure what he was thinking and her stomach knotted. But eventually he nodded, his enthusiasm around twenty per cent of what it had

been. 'Okay. Let's think time management, then. How about one-hour blocks? One hour to snorkel. One hour to travel there and back, shower… One hour for work?'

'Okay. I'll get my things ready.'

He nodded, but the oomph had leached out of him. 'I'll take the pups up to Tina, then meet you at the garages—apparently there's every kind of vehicle we might need in there.'

Looked like she didn't have a choice.

This was the worst damned idea he'd had in years.

Jake watched as Lola discarded her T-shirt and shorts and stood a little away from him on the sand, with a towel tightly wrapped around herself. Underneath, he knew, she was wearing a black bikini that covered her curves well enough, but did nothing to hide her great figure. He swallowed, trying not to look too closely…but in the end it didn't really matter, as his body was hell-bent on reacting anyway. His mouth watered at the thought of her perfect mouth, and his fingers craved to smooth down her wind-wild hair. Never mind the tight clutch low down in his belly that had him turning away from her. Thank God there was cold water close by.

Working would have been a much better idea but here he was, instead, with a reluctant accomplice and a serious case of hot lust. Why he'd even bothered to invite her he didn't know. Playing hooky for once in his thirty-three years had seemed like a good idea when talking to Tina. Harmless.

In truth, he should have stayed back at the house and tried to catch Cameron for that conversation he still hadn't had with her. It had been such a temptation to talk to Lola about the pregnancy— obviously confidentiality meant he never could— but he got the feeling Cameron needed more than him looking out for her.

'Have you got a wetsuit? Rash guard? The sun's fierce, you don't want to get burnt,' he growled at Lola, taking a step away from her. He didn't want to have to rub sunscreen on to that gorgeous body, or they'd never actually get into the ocean.

And what he needed more than anything was a dose of cold seawater to sluice away the physical ache he had for her—especially seeing her right now; lush red curls against creamy pale skin, breasts that threatened to break free from flimsy string masquerading as a bikini, and a waist that looked the perfect size for his hands to grip.

'Yes, boss. Here.' She turned and held up a pink neoprene jacket and put it on, zipping up the front. *Thank God.*

He couldn't get his head around the fact that the kiss had seemed real and wanted on both sides, and yet now she wanted to be anywhere other than with him. But he'd got the message, and she was right. There were too many reasons to prevent him getting involved with anyone, let alone a woman who had such a serious effect on his equilibrium.

'Tina said that over by the rocks was the best place to start. There's some coral there, so take care not to stand on it, we don't want to damage it.' And with that he turned and made his way down towards the water, fins and mask in hand.

But she was with him in two strides.

'So, isn't this the best look ever?' Laughing, Lola dragged her mask over her face and made piggy eyes at him as she pulled the mouth tube into her mouth.

Actually, it was a pretty damned sexy look, and

he was shocked by how much he wanted to haul her to him, even with a plastic mask on. So he dived deep into the clear, cool water and got on with fish-spotting.

Jake was always surprised at the serenity of the ocean; all that busy activity down there, yet little sound save for the ebb and flow of waves and the echo of his heartbeat in his ears. The sun warmed his back as a whole new world opened up below him. The little underwater gardens were teeming with life and there was enough interest to grab his attention away from the hunger Lola had started in his gut.

They followed the curve of the bay out west, floating and bobbing with the tide, popping up for air as and when they needed it, agreeing on a course to follow, then swimming and watching and pointing at the sea life. Lola was an excellent snorkeller, easily excited by the large black manta ray gliding along the seabed and the schools of pretty purple and electric-blue fish that darted back and forth in front of them.

Then she kicked away to follow a shoal of bright yellow spotted ones, and for a few moments he was alone—just skimming along the top of the water looking down into the rhythmic swaying of the seaweed on the coral.

His heart rate slowed, and for the first time since he'd set foot in the Caribbean he began to relax. The cool water washed over him and with it his sense of equilibrium and purpose was renewed. It was only a few days in the Bahamas, they could rub along together for that, fill their days with activities and surround themselves with other people. Soon enough they'd be back to LA and their normal lives. After that, the filming would swiftly wrap up and he'd have no reason to see her again. With time, he hoped, this ache would die and she'd just be a quaint memory. Like the other women who'd flitted in and out of his life.

It would all work out fine.

He didn't know how long they'd been there, but suddenly the water turned choppy. Expecting the wave wash of a boat or a jet ski, he lifted his head out of the water and came face-to-face with a grinning Lola. She ripped the mouth tube from her lips and pointed out to sea. 'Look! Look! Dolphins.'

Sure enough, a pod of bottlenose dolphins was

diving and playing in the deeper reef. 'Oh, yeah. Pretty cool.'

As she trod water she gripped his shoulder. 'Cool? It's flipping amazing. Look at them, showing off, playing together. Do you think we could swim with them? D'you think?'

'You'll have to be quick.' And before he could argue she'd grabbed his hand and was half swimming and half dragging him through the waves, trying to catch them up. For little more than a few minutes the dolphins gave them a magical show of their skills, corkscrewing over and over, darting underneath their legs and popping up behind them. One of them took a liking to Lola and pushed his nose at her. She reached out and touched him before he darted away. He returned twice and played the same teasing game—pushing his nose at her, waiting for her to reach and then disappearing into the foam. Then, just as quickly as they'd appeared, they were all off in a display of enthusiasm, swimming faster than humanly possible and disappearing into the distance.

'Wow...I can't... This is so...' Lola stopped and grasped his hand again, coughing as she took off her mask. The outlines of the rubber seal had marked her pretty face, but she was grinning widely, tears shimmering in her eyes. She looked so damned beautiful it made his chest constrict. 'I don't know what to say. That was… Oh, my God! Dolphins. That was so amazing.'

'Yeah. Very cool.' He took off his mask too and affected an English accent. 'Pretty flipping amazing, actually.' Like she was, with bright golden flashes in her dark brown eyes, her hair slicked back, droplets of water falling from her eyelashes. A mouth that he ached to taste all over again.

'Yes, it is. All of it. Everything…' Her voice cracked. She looked at him as she held onto his shoulder, her legs working beneath the surface to keep her upright, while something passed between them. Something electric, something real and hot. Everything felt as it had when they'd kissed, the charge in the air was the same—an almost tangible shimmer between them.

But that couldn't be right, because she'd said… What had she said? That she was messing things up for him. But here she wasn't messing up anything, here she was making the trip a whole lot more bearable. But he was useless at reading signals, especially in ten feet of water when words and actions didn't gel. 'Lola, we should probably go now.'

'But—'

'We need to get back. An hour for each, we agreed.' He made a start for the shore, leaving the cooler depths behind and entering the warmer water where it was almost shallow enough to stand up, had it not been for the coral gardens beneath their feet.

'Wait. Stop a minute.' Panting, she caught up with him, grasped his arm. 'Thank you for bringing me here. I'm sorry I was so hard to convince. I don't want to get in the way of your work. I know how important that is to you.'

'Yeah, but you can't work all the time. People keep telling me.' He reached and wiped some water from her cheek. It was cold out here but heat exploded through him. All the more reason to get the hell out. 'But we can't put it off forever either. We'd better make a start back.'

'Stop.' She reached for his jaw and ran her palm over his cheek. 'Do we need to think about work right now?'

Her legs made little swirling kicks around him.

He could feel the rhythmic movement, and a need to have her wrap those legs around his hips almost overwhelmed him.

He should have turned and swam away then. He should have listened to the voice in his head reminding him of what she'd said. But he did neither. Instead, he put his hand on her waist and pulled her closer. And, yes—it was a perfect fit for his palm. 'What do you want to think about?'

'Actually, I don't feel much like thinking at all.' She looked up from beneath long eyelashes adorned with droplets like a hundred tiny diamonds highlighting the flashes of colour in her eyes and the intensity of need.

His heart was raging a wild tattoo in his chest. Because even though he was lame at reading signals, he was pretty sure he knew what this one was saying. And, for the record, Lola was nothing like the others. She was special. Unique. 'What do you feel like doing?'

'I want to kiss you again.' She wriggled closer into his open arms and slanted her wet mouth against his, and all thoughts of work and conflicting signals, and all the reasons to stop fled from his brain. He dragged her hard against him and kissed her back.

She tasted of salt and the sea, she tasted fresh and hot and hungry. As she entwined her legs with his he pushed his fingers into her hair, cradled her head and relished the press of her glorious curves against him. Her hand ran down his back as she moaned into his mouth, fingernails grasping at his skin.

Slowly he nipped along her bottom lip then kissed along her collarbone to the soft hollow at her throat, and she tilted her head back and laughed.

'God, Jake, I've been dreaming about this.'

'You too?' He tugged the zip on her neoprene and slowly freed her breasts, slid his palm over one as he took her mouth again. Beneath his fingers her nipples contracted to tight buds and he coaxed them, first gently stroking then—reluctantly leaving her mouth—he was licking them against the rise and fall of the ocean.

It *was* like a crazy dream—a beautiful woman, a deserted beach, the reach and grasp of a delicious need that spiralled through him.

'Oh, yes.' She pulled his mouth from her nipple

and cupped his face, anchoring him to her, deepening the kiss, hard and wet, pulsing in time with the waves. The kiss became urgent, the need for her almost frantic. He was so hard. So hard for her and she knew it as she wriggled against him and groaned with pleasure.

Laughing, she wrapped her legs around his hips, and as she did so, something wrapped tight around his heart and tugged. The light sound of her carefree laughter, the sway of the ocean waves, the rush of adrenalin and heat filled him with more than desire. He wanted her, too much.

It would have been so easy to slide back her bikini bottoms and thrust into her there, but reality began to seep into his brain. There was no future in this, and Lola was the kind of woman who would want the fairy-tale future in the end. Regardless of what she may say or do now, he couldn't promise her anything apart from a good time and a goodbye.

She was fresh and untainted, she was something new and good. And, when it came down to it, he wasn't. Not where women were concerned. He didn't want them to cloud his vision, to distract him. He had a lot to achieve—a debt to repay. He didn't want to have to consider another person.

Lola deserved to be considered.

He pulled away and held her wrists. 'Lola, we need to stop this.'

'Yes, God, my legs are killing me, treading water. Let's get to dry land…and then…you know…there's not a soul on the beach and I see a secluded place…'

He shook his head. 'Let's talk once we get to the beach.'

'Talk?' She almost flinched, the hit to her gut was visible, but she slowly absorbed it. Her smile slipped as she realised what he was saying. For a second he thought she was going to agree with him, but she hit her open palm hard on the top of the water so spray arced over him. 'You know what, Jake? You are so damned annoying.'

Then she started to swim hard towards the shore.

After a minute or so she stopped and turned to him, breathless, angry, legs kicking beneath the surface. 'I don't get it. I don't get why you do all that and then listen to whatever it was in your head telling you to stop. Because I know you want to kiss me, Jake. I know you want to fool around and I do too. So why the hell—? Ow! Oh. Wow.' She gasped sharply, then again as her face contorted in pain and she started to thrash under the water. 'Go. To. Hell—Ow! *Ow!*'

'Lola? What's wrong?'

'I—? Leave. Me. Alone.' She bobbed under the water, grasping at her leg. When she resurfaced she was blinking back tears, pressing her hand to her mouth and trying to stay afloat.

Jake's heart hammered. 'What's wrong? Lola, what's happened?'

'Something stung me. Bit me? Ow...' Her face was pinched and he could see she was fighting pain. 'Oh, what the hell do you care anyway?'

'Quite a damned lot, actually.' The reality of that gave him a powerful thump to his solar plexus. This was not the time for arguing or playing stupid games.

CHAPTER SEVEN

'CALM DOWN. TAKE A deep breath. Breathe, Lola. And again. That's it. Good. It's okay. I've got you.' Jake's arms wrapped round her as he kicked hard towards the beach. Her leg felt as if someone was holding a hot poker against it, the burn ripped through the flesh to the bone. She clung on to his shoulders as he powered through the waves.

She just wanted the pain to stop. *I will not cry.* 'Jellyfish? D'you think it's a jellyfish? Are there more? Don't get stung too.' She had to shout over the roar of waves and the rush of white noise in her head, though it came out like a panicked, high-pitched squeal.

'I didn't see anything swimming around… But, then, I was distracted…' He hauled in oxygen, breathing hard as he bore the weight of the two of them. 'Could be anything. Lola, keep still.'

'It hurts.'

'I know it does.' And he was there for her, holding her, saving her. Regardless of what he'd said about the kissing. He was there, she'd remember that—once she'd got over the pain and the humiliation of being rejected. *Again.*

In no time at all they reached the beach and he laid her on the sand at the water's edge and bathed her leg with cooling seawater. His eyes had lost the heat she'd seen before, but there was something else there—concern, hesitation. 'How's it feeling now?'

'Okay. And stop being so bloody nice to me.' It made things a million times worse, and made her like him even more.

'First time anyone's ever complained about me being considerate.' His tone was kind and patient, in contrast to hers.

'That's because you're showing me your nice side, but I know you have a bad side. And, no, it's not okay any more. Every time you stop bathing it hurts even more. I think I'll keep the water on it.' She bit her lip and shuffled deeper into the water, scanning first for any rogue jellyfish that might have followed them. 'My heart's racing really fast.'

'It's probably just adrenalin from the shock—

you'll be fine. Just sit a while. Try more deep breaths. In…slowly…and now out…that's it.' Calmly he took her hand, pressed two fingers just below her thumb and focused. After way longer than a minute he was still holding her wrist, his palm stroking her skin. Now her heart was beating erratically for an altogether different reason. Again in that considerate tone he said, 'Here, lean against me. Keep your foot in the water until you feel you can stand. Then I'll take you to a clinic.'

'Clinic? I don't have time… We've got to get back. Cameron needs us.'

'Cameron will have to wait.'

'Seriously? Have you tried telling her to do anything she doesn't…?' But the searing burn was turning now into an aggravating itch. She wanted to tear at her skin. When she looked down she saw huge red welts and blisters starting to appear. So she leaned against him anyway, taking strength from his heat, her fist coiled into his. 'It's starting to itch like crazy. Don't suppose you have jellyfish antidotes back at the lodge?'

'Sure, I have something for every kind of emergency; polar-bear bait, black widow spider antivenin. Zombie-killer stakes.' He pushed her matted hair away from her face with his free hand and pressed a kiss on to the top of her head— as he would to a child. 'No, oddly, I don't have jellyfish antidote, even if there is such a thing, but usually you just need cold water and something acidic. Seriously, we've got to get it seen by someone. If it was a jellyfish—and it may have been something else—we need to get the right treatment. Some of them are deadly.'

'And now you're making me feel so much better about this. But apart from wanting to rip my skin off, I think I'll take a chance on walking.' She let him haul her up from the sand and watched while he gathered their things together, then she let him half carry her as she hopped towards the motor scooters. 'Maybe the cool rush of air as I'm scooting along will help.'

'You are not driving that scooter on your own, Lola. You're shaking; you won't be able to steer. Climb on the front of mine. I'll send someone to pick yours up later.' Then he made a quick phone call, flicked his cell phone back into his bag and indicated for her to sit in front of him, old-fashioned side-saddle style.

'I... Oh, okay.' She didn't want to, but she

did anyway, sliding her arms around his waist, pressing her head against the solid wall of his chest, breathing in the scent of man and elements and some flowery fragrance from the beautiful blooms all around them, but she didn't care about that. All she could think of was the pain and the itch and the kiss and the way he'd felt, so hard, so hungry for her. The way he'd turned away from her, denying what he'd so obviously wanted.

And the way he'd looked at her when she'd been hurt, as if he'd do everything in his power to help her. If he hadn't been so nice she'd have bawled him out all the more for stopping the kissing. Because here she was, with a guy who was the hottest thing on two legs and who also had a damned conscience.

'That's fire coral rash, pretty sure, Dr Jake.' Tina was standing over the couch, hands on her ample hips, peering at Lola's leg. Thankfully the painkillers were kicking in and the intense burning was subsiding, but the itch was driving her mad and there were still angry red welts on her ankle. Not to mention swelling.

And outright humiliation. Typical. Only she

would be in the middle of paradise and get attacked by a man-eating plant.

'Fire coral?' Jake frowned. 'What's that?'

'Looks like coral, but has venom,' Tina explained. 'She'll live. Vinegar to kill the barbs. Then you can tweezer them out.'

'Great. I saw some vinegar in the kitchen and I'll go grab my medical kit.' Jake nodded. He'd been nothing but focused on her comfort since the second she'd screamed at him in the sea. 'She needs a hot drink for the shock. If you can get that sorted for me, please.'

'Sure. She looks mighty pale.' Tina shook her head and frowned.

He frowned too. 'She'll be okay with rest and something to raise her blood sugar.'

'Hey. I am here.' Tired of being talked over, Lola managed a smile. 'You can talk *to* me if you like. Tina, yes, I'd love a drink if you have time to make me one. And, no, Jake, you're not going anywhere near me with vinegar and tweezers. I can do it myself.'

'Really? You can twist your body at that kind of an angle and rip nematocysts out like a pro? This I've got to see. Wait right there.'

He dashed out of the room as Lola leaned back on the sofa, closed her eyes and groaned. She did not want to be beholden to him and she did not want him touching her again with all that kind consideration. Really, they needed to talk, not touch. Touching brought about way too many hot thoughts and not enough searing reality.

She didn't need reminding that her particular searing reality was that she was here to work and not mess about with a doctor, no matter how much her body had other ideas. And now, accompanying Cameron to the location shoot was looking pretty touch and go. 'Oh…why me?'

'Because, Miss Bennett, you didn't have a full wetsuit on.'

Lola had forgotten the housekeeper was still there. 'Oh, sorry, Tina, I was thinking about how I was going to manage to work this afternoon.'

'You won't, no arguing.' It was Jake again, back with them and holding his large black medical bag, which he set down on the floor. 'Tina, it's okay, we can manage here, thanks. I don't want to take up any more of your time…except I'd be grateful if you could take the dogs for a while. Lola, you're going to stay there and rest.'

Lola sat up. 'I can't do that. There's too much—'

'Shh. I'm the doctor and you'll do what I say. I'll go with Cameron. Once we've got the barbs out you can get some rest. You've had a bad shock.' Not as shocking as necking in an ocean, to be honest, but there it was. He lifted her swollen leg onto a footstool, on which he'd laid out a dressing pack and drape, then he crouched down. 'Now, this is going to sting so I'll go slowly.'

'It won't sting if I do it.' She reached for the tweezers, bent her legs and shuffled so she could see the barbs. She didn't want him to see her frustrated tears or her weakest moments. She just wanted him to go and leave her to recover in peace.

He watched, eyebrows peaked. 'And pray tell me how you'll stop the sting if I can't?'

'I don't know. Just let me do it and stop asking questions.'

'Okay. Go right ahead.' He rocked back on his heels and smirked as she tried to reach, couldn't quite, and twisted some more. She got a deep ache low in her back. And still the barbs were stuck in her leg. 'Go on, Lola, I'm waiting.'

'Okay, clever clogs, you do it then.' She all but threw the tweezers at him.

He rocked forward and grabbed them. 'Stop me any time, there's no hurry.'

'No problem.' She wasn't sure where this big brave act was coming from, but in truth she didn't want to owe him anything or to let him see how upset she felt. She was a grown-up, smart adult woman—she could deal with this. 'I'll be fine.'

His eyes were gentle and warm as he smiled. 'Sure you will. You can handle anything, Lola.'

'Yep.' At least one of them had some faith in her. She sucked in a breath as he touched her leg, sending shivers of pain through her calf. She would not shout. She would not cry.

He paused, tweezers in mid-air, and it was worse to see compassion mixed with teasing in his eyes. 'It is okay to scream. I have ear plugs somewhere.'

'Get on with it, man. The suspense is killing me more than the damned venom ever will.'

The next few minutes passed in a blur of angry stinging, fierce tensing of muscles she hadn't known she had and almost ripping the stuffing from the chair arm. When Jake felt satisfied he'd removed every barb, he smoothed cream over the now very puce ankle and calf and gave her another dose of painkiller. 'You did well. Lie back and get some rest. I'm going up to the house to talk Cameron into letting you stay here.'

'Good luck with that. I doubt she'll be happy. It's okay. Give me a few minutes for the pain to calm down and I'll come with you.'

'You'll stay right there, missy.'

'Or what?'

'Or you'll get a spanking.' His hand was on the door but instead of leaving he looked at her and shook his head. 'I shouldn't have said that.'

She smiled on a sigh. 'Promises…promises.'

'Lola…' There was a warning in his voice but a glint in his eyes.

'I know, I know. Timing. Work. Stuff. Life. I get it. If you look for excuses you'll find them.'

'They're everywhere, Lola. I don't need to look. Now, I'm going to tell Cameron that you have to stay here.'

'My money's on an immediate departure to the set for all of us, dogs included.'

But Cameron, it seemed, had other ideas. Very surprising.

Apparently she insisted that her assistant stay at the lodge and that Jake stay with her. A situation they both found irritating. More Jake, it seemed.

He slumped down in the chair opposite Lola, grumbling, 'She was surrounded by Alfredo's guests and just wafted her hand and told me to stay with you as if it was no big deal that a top neurosurgeon was wasting his time here—and I couldn't get to talk to her privately. She demanded I come all this way, cancel my clinics and rearrange my schedule, and now she doesn't even need me to go with her, and won't let me talk to her.'

Lola lifted her head from the couch then laid it back again when the room started to spin a little. 'I think you're just her insurance policy. She hasn't been feeling great over the last few months on that stupid diet. She probably just needs to know you're close by in case of emergency. You're here, filming's only a few miles away, she can call if she needs you.'

'Which was exactly what she said to me.'

'Why do you want to go anyway? Seems to me you don't want to be here in the first place, so an afternoon off would suit you just fine.'

'It's my job.' He shrugged, pulling out his laptop. 'Right, if you're okay with it I'll log into the clinic intranet and get some work done. I can't sit around doing nothing.'

'Me neither.' Lola swung her legs from the stool and tried to stand. It was relatively easy to bear weight, but the pain knocked the wind out of her lungs. 'Oof.'

'What do you think you're doing?' He glared at her over the top of his computer screen.

'Going to get my phone. I'll do some ringing around, sort out a dress for Cameron for the after-shoot dinner tomorrow night.'

'All that luggage and she didn't bring a dress?'

'Of course she did. I packed more than enough clothes for a whole month. But there are some fabulous Bahamian designers and she wants to try their clothes. I call, they send. She wears. Or not. It's routine. She could make them a lot of money being seen in one of their creations. Top one on my list is Evelyn Rice—some of her dresses were worn at awards ceremonies earlier in the year and—'

'Okay.' Jake came over to her and made her sit back down, his hand slipping around her waist.

He was comfortable around her body when there wasn't the immediate threat of a kiss, it seemed. His voice was soothing. 'I'll get your phone. You can make one call. One. Then you need to do something that isn't work. Solitaire? Knitting? Your script? Yes. Your script. This is legitimate sick time, which means no work—just relaxation.'

'You know, you can be quite bossy when you try.' But she had to agree it would be nice to sit and do something for herself. The extra-strong painkillers had started to make her head feel woozy and her limbs like melting honey—limpid and weak. She felt as if she was sinking and flying at the same time, which was doubly weird. 'My phone's in my beach bag and my script's on my dresser in the bedroom.'

'By the look of you, those meds are kicking in. Very soon you won't want to do anything, you'll be asleep in five minutes.'

When he came back she was still trying to find a comfortable position on the sofa. 'The cushion doesn't feel right.' And she was indeed very tired. Very tired indeed.

'Hold on.' Jake put her phone and her script on

the arm of the sofa and sat down next to her to plump up the cushion. 'Better?'

'Not really. But thank you for trying and for talking to Cameron. I know she doesn't mean to be difficult, she's just learnt to be like that. She can be really nice—she gave me a dress once, just because I liked it. But I get how everyone sees the bad in her when she gets so demanding. If I could just sell my screenplay then I wouldn't have to stay... Where did you put it?' Why was she only hearing her own voice? Was she talking too much? She probably was, but she couldn't stop even though it was getting harder to control her mouth movements. She had to concentrate to say the words. 'Ah, there it is. Thank you.'

'Have you sent it to him to read yet?'

'My dad?' Her heart thumped once at the thought of what she'd done but then...she didn't feel so bad right now... 'No. I can't. I haven't... I should. But, oh, Jake, there's too much... It's hard...to explain...I will, though. I will send it to him...' How to start that conversation? *I know you think I'm in LA making the most of Cameron's connections, but I lied and I keep on lying...* 'I'll send it tomorrow. Maybe...I might have to...'

Jake ran his finger over her cheek. 'Now I understand why he calls you a chatterbox. One tiny relaxant and you're in full throttle. Let me know when you need me to reply, because the gaps you're leaving aren't big enough for me to get a word in.'

'Oops, sorry.'

'No need to apologise. Now read.' Smiling, Jake lifted her leg and she kind of swung sideways and landed against his arm. Without thinking twice, she snuggled under and into his armpit. He was so warm and strong. Comfortable... And he smelt delicious. Her eyes started to close, her heart slowed a little and it was so tempting just to lie against him and... She should really look at her script, but she didn't have the energy...

He gave her a little nudge. 'Lola. Lola...don't go to sleep here.'

'Hmm?'

His voice was by her ear, warm and soft. 'Maybe you should go to bed. You'll be more comfortable.'

'Hmm? No. I'm fine.' There was an opportunity for more innuendo there, but she couldn't move her mouth enough to say anything much. It was as if her brain was on a go-slow. She just wanted to lie here in his arms and let the pain drift away. 'Can't walk… Stay right here?'

When he didn't answer she let herself fall further down into the black hole. When he nuzzled the top of her head she spiralled further and further… He was very close. Nice and close and warm. Her body started to tingle, starting first in her gut but then spreading through her, to her breasts and down low, deep inside. Half asleep and half turned on. No—all turned on, in a drowsy, calm, warm kind of way. Sex would be delicious right now. Sex with Jake would be more than delicious.

She managed to twist herself so she was facing him. His mouth was only inches from hers. His eyes glittered with concern and desire, his Adam's apple bobbed as he swallowed. 'Lola—'

Again a warning. She knew exactly what she wanted to do right now, and wondered if he thought the same thing. 'Jake. I know you said—'

'Hush.' He placed a finger over her mouth. 'You need some rest.'

She curled her hand around his finger and drew it away. Then she leaned close and pressed her mouth against his, because she couldn't not. Because she knew it was what they both wanted. And for a brief moment she felt his hesitation, heard his low groan before his free hand cupped her cheek and he kissed her back, soft and gentle. She reached for his face, for the soft touch of his skin; she wanted to be sheathed in his scent, to taste him over and over and over.

This time the kiss went deeper than passion, to somewhere beyond the rabid desperation she felt inside. It stoked something fierce, something rare and beautiful. Something precious.

She didn't want this to stop; she curled the back of her hand against his cheek and melted into the press of his lips against hers, into the dance of his tongue, the tight clutch of her stomach. This was something. He was something. Something important. Something good. For the first time ever she felt soul-deep that this was right.

When he drew away Jake was shaking and there were deep lines across his forehead. He looked unsettled, spooked.

Worse, she felt as if someone had taken her lifeline away. 'I'm not going crazy, am I? There is something here? You do want this, right?' She knew her words were coming out a little slurred, as if her mouth was full of cotton-wool. But she wanted to know…needed to know. He'd said they'd talk, well, now she was going to say a few things… 'Because I want to kiss you. And maybe more. Some more…yes, more.' She laid her hand on his chest, felt the reassuring beat of his heart under her fingers. There was something about Jake that was different from any other man she'd ever known. There was a quiet strength to him—one that irritated her slightly as he fought the attraction. There was a calmness there. He was funny and beautiful to look at. He made her feel good about herself. He made her think that anything was possible.

He made her lose track of her thinking—and that wasn't always such a good thing. Because she had to keep her mind focused on her goals. She didn't want to fall for him—but maybe it was already too late. Right now she was so laconic she didn't care.

There was a long pause while he looked at her. Sin flashed across his gaze. 'Yes. Yes, I do want to kiss you again, Lola, and more. But wanting and doing are different things. You're hurting now, and pretty much flying high on meds, you don't know what you're doing—and, to be brutally honest, neither do I. You need to sleep it all off. Things will look different when you wake up.'

His rejection should have hurt, but it didn't touch her. Because she knew. Knew he wanted her. Knew this was right. She couldn't stop looking at his mouth. She wanted to feel his mouth on her skin, on her body. Everywhere. 'Why do you keep pushing me away?'

'Because I wouldn't be good for you.'

Oh, you would. So damned good. But she had to admit that her vision had started to blur at the edges and she was feeling quite strange. 'I think I can decide what's good for me. I think sex with you would be amazing—'

His growl was low and almost feral as he edged away from her. 'So do I, Lola. Which is exactly why we're not going to do it.'

CHAPTER EIGHT

THE AIR WAS cooler when she woke, alone on the sofa, her body contorted, her limbs still limp, her head aching just a little. Her mouth was dry. And she was sure she was supposed to be doing something important, but all she could remember was lying in Jake's heat and how safe she'd felt.

It was going dark too. Almost six o'clock.

She'd been asleep for hours, way too long.

Whoa, shoot. She was supposed to have phoned Evelyn Rice's office and organised some clothes. And the beauty therapist…damn, damn, damn.

Her head was clearing now, very quickly. Unfortunately. There was no soft-focus buzz to make the neglect of her duties appear in any way warm and fuzzy. She reached for her phone.

But it was gone. As was her script. She jumped to her feet. Wobbled a little on her bad leg. Righted herself. What in hell had she been thinking, sleeping for so long as if she hadn't a care in the world?

What had he given her for the pain that had wiped her brain of any sense? 'Jake? Jake?'

He wasn't in the kitchen, bedrooms…the bathrooms were empty. She started to wander outside, but met him and the dogs in the hallway. He'd changed out of beach clothes and wore a navy collared T-shirt that clung interestingly to his biceps, and tan shorts that made a perfect gift of his backside. And he gripped three leads tightly in his fist. 'Hey, you're awake. Get down, Butter or Jelly, or whoever you are. Stop fussing. We've been for a walk. I think Tina was getting just a little tired of them. Cameron's still on set.'

Lola was still a little drowsy, but her head was no longer filled with mush. She bent to stroke the dogs, gave them all the kisses they needed, then stood. Wobbled a little. 'Why did you let me sleep so long?'

Jake held her arms at her sides and looked her up and down, steadied her. 'You needed it. Your body told you what it needed. You've been working hard, you were in shock…'

'I was drugged.'

He laughed. 'Lightweight. Seriously, they

weren't even strong. How're you feeling? You seem to be walking okay.'

She peered down at her leg. It was still red and swollen, but not as raw as it had been. The pain had definitely subsided and whatever cream he'd put on had helped reduce the itch. Reduce, not obliterate. 'Better. But I haven't time to think about that. I need to phone Evelyn Rice and arrange some clothes for tomorrow. But, damn, she's probably left already, and I only have the workshop number.'

'No need.' He walked her back through to the kitchen and let the dogs off their leads, and after they'd scoffed some biscuits they scampered through the open-plan space to the lounge area, climbed onto their favourite rattan sofa and began preening. Just like their 'mother'.

Talking of which… 'But—I have to—Cameron asked me—'

'Wait.' Jake opened the fridge, lifted out a bottle and filled a glass with iced water then handed it to Lola. 'Drink this. Okay, I've already phoned Miss Rice. It's all sorted.'

'You called her? Oh, my God, what on earth did you say?' This was it. She was fired. Gone.

Back to London. Regretting everything…except the part where she'd kissed Jake. Twice.

Whatever, she was doomed.

He grinned, obviously pleased with himself. 'I explained what the issue was, and that I hadn't a clue what I was doing. She took pity on me. She was delighted Cameron wanted to sample her clothes and we guessed her size. She's sending an assortment of this season's garments over tonight, different sizes just in case.'

Lola tiptoed to kiss his cheek, but thought better of it. The last time she'd kissed him things had gone downhill pretty quickly. 'Great, thanks. That's brilliant. You are brilliant.'

'I know.'

'And very modest too. So the only other major thing I need to do today is arrange a beautician for tomorrow evening for before the dinner.'

This time he gave her a very satisfied look. 'Done.'

'What?' He was a revelation.

'Evelyn recommended someone. I called, she's fitting Cameron in. In fact, she's rearranged her whole day for *that divine woman*. Her words, not mine.'

This time she did give him a quick peck on the cheek and neither of them seemed to mind. 'Double brilliant. Thank you. You're a lifesaver.'

'I know.'

'But what I don't understand is why.' To think that only a few days ago she'd never even met the man, and now he was doing her job for her, tending to her leg. And not trying to sleep with her… Maybe he was just an altogether good guy.

Apart from not trying to sleep with her…

'To save your ass. The last thing you needed was to make a drug-slurred call to a top designer. Not a great look. Now…' He took her hand and walked her out to the deck. In the distance someone was playing soca music, light and lyrical. 'Sit down. Chef is sending dinner over in ten minutes. Watch the sunset…or something. I'll just check on the dogs.'

'Oh. Wow. Yes.' She gazed out and wondered whether the drugs were having an effect on her vision—because the view was breathtaking. It looked like someone had taken a paintbrush and daubed the brightest colours they could find right across the horizon.

The sky met the ocean in a deep molten orange

that reflected across the water. A bright yellow globe dipped into the sea and shimmered almost golden. To her left, palm trees swayed in silhouette, black against the ombre haze. And there, just in front of her, were two large torches, flames flickering in the gentle breeze, and a table set for two with candles and white linen.

Her phone was there, too, next to her script. The pages were held down with pebbles at the place where he'd stopped reading. The End.

All this had happened while she'd been asleep?

'The more time I spend here the more impressed I am.' He pulled out a chair and indicated for her to sit. 'The dogs are fine. Asleep. Cameron's busy. Sit down.'

'You read my script?' She sat. Heat burnt her cheeks. She might as well have been naked in front of him. Worse. What could be worse than laying open her naked self to him?

Ah, yes. Laying open her heart. That was something she didn't want to do. Flirting and fun were one thing, but she didn't need him to know about the clutch of her heart when she'd kissed him. She didn't want him to know how much she admired him. Some things she had to keep to herself to protect her heart from the fallout.

He sat opposite her and was about to speak when the chef arrived with a tray of food. Lobster, crab, potatoes, fruit. An amazing array of delicious local delicacies. She turned down wine and stuck to water, not wanting to mix the painkillers with alcohol and befuddle her head even more.

After a couple of mouthfuls and uninhibited groans of delight at the fresh flavours, he put his knife and fork down.

'So, yes, I did read your script.' He was unabashed, as if reading her words hadn't been like peering into her soul.

'And?'

'It's excellent. Really, I think you should do something with it.' He drank some rosé wine, took up his cutlery again. 'But what do I know? I'm a doctor. You need an expert opinion, not mine. Show it to Cameron, she's an expert on tap.'

Lola almost choked on her lobster. 'I couldn't do that. I'd rather die than press it on her and beg her to read it. Believe me, she wouldn't anyway, she has far too much to do. She doesn't even know I write.'

'Well, she should. That story deserves a home. You're right, it is surprisingly funny. Although I shouldn't be surprised—it's just an extension of you. With all the things you are—funny, smart, witty, brave.'

'Wow. Thank you. Thank you so much.' She felt a surge of confidence. 'I don't think I'll ever believe it's ready to go out into the big wide world.'

'Email it to your dad.'

This time she felt the thuds in her heart go on and on at the mention of her dad. But she wasn't going to have that conversation with Jake. 'Yeah…maybe.'

'Tomorrow?'

'Pushy.'

His tone got serious. 'What are you waiting for? You want a career in this? Yes? You've given up everything to come out here for *this*?' He stabbed his finger at the paper on the table. 'But you're still at first base. You won't get on if you don't *do* things. You know the old saying—if you want something to work for you, you have to *make* it work. Right?'

'Right.' She was almost carried along with his enthusiasm. Sure, she was dedicated, ambitious, hard-working…but putting herself out there? There was too much at stake for her right now. He was talking about things he had no knowledge of. 'Are you this demanding on everyone?'

'Usually just myself.'

'Why?'

He looked down at his food. 'We work hard… Look, my parents didn't have much, but they taught me that you can achieve anything if you're prepared to put the hours in. Now, about that script…'

It didn't escape her notice that he'd changed the subject back to her as soon as he could. Talking about his family clearly wasn't a favourite thing of his. Well, snap to that. 'Yes. Okay. I'll get it out there as soon as I can.'

'Send a copy to me too so I can take another look at the medical scenes. Soup them up a bit. You're in a prime position to change your life, Lola.'

'Yes, yes, I am.' He was good at this—voicing the feelings she'd arrived with in LA. 'Have you always been this in control of your own life? Planning world domination?'

He grinned. 'Like I said, my career's fine, thanks. Going right according to plan. No need to analyse that any further.'

'So what do you do when you're *not* working?'

'Like that happens.'

'You must do something. You can't work all the time.' At his shrug she realised he really, truly, probably did. 'You don't have hobbies?'

'I work out. Hike. Surf, if I get a chance. Haven't done that for a while. I've been building my practice—these things don't just happen. I—well, I work, Lola. Although sometimes to the detriment of other things—I understand that. You have to make sacrifices.' It was almost as if he'd just realised that he didn't do anything else—as if the realisation was finally seeping into his brain, and what exactly that meant for his life. Then he smiled. 'Oh, and I juggle, but that's more for relaxation. Well, I used to—it's been a while. Years, actually. Probably a decade, if I'm honest. So, okay, I admit I'm a sad case of a workaholic—I do all the things I tell my juniors not to do. But I have to work, no one's going to carry me the rest of my life. Where I end up is up to me. No one else.'

And she wondered what he meant by that—but sensed he was reluctant to talk about it, so she tried to keep things light. 'So you juggle, like with the oranges earlier? That's a strange thing to do.'

His eyebrows rose. 'Unusual, yes. Strange—not so. It's very therapeutic, especially if your brain's stuck in one thing and you want to move on. I was part of a study when I was at med school. We were testing whether learning a new skill could promote white and grey matter growth in the brain. It does, by the way. It also helps you focus and relax, helps posture and co-ordination…and usually makes people smile.'

'I might have known it would have some connection to work.'

'Of course. Plus, it's a great babe magnet.'

She laughed. 'Why? How?'

'That's my secret.'

'Tell me?'

'No.'

'Okay, then, teach me?'

'Sure. Why not?' Standing, he took hold of her arm and they went inside to the kitchen. He picked up two oranges from the fruit bowl, one in each hand, and threw them up in the air. She was mesmerised by the fluidity of his movements, the flex of his hands, the primed, yet relaxed stance. His smile. She was mesmerised by him.

He caught the oranges in one hand, held one out to her. 'Start like this. Just up and down. That's right. Now, try two. Throw from one hand to the other in an arc shape. Copy me.'

She did as she was told and copied him as he threw first one orange, then added in another so they crossed in mid throw. 'Easy!'

'Okay... Now try using your non-dominant hand. That's the tricky bit.'

'Oops.' One orange landed on the floor in a splat.

He laughed. 'Not quite ready for flames yet...'

'You juggle with fire?'

'I have. I can. Try it like this.' He stood behind her and captured her between his arms, his hands cupping hers as they threw the oranges into the air. She leaned against him and he held her weight, his breath coming easily against her neck. She could feel the hard wall of his chest against her back, could smell his scent, and she suddenly felt more alive and more clear-headed than she had all day.

Arousal snaked up her spine, through her veins. Her heart began to beat faster. She wanted to turn around and press herself against him, to feel him naked against her. Her hands shook as she held the oranges. His words were in her ear, on her neck, in her hair. 'Lola…your turn now, on your own. I'll stay here ready to catch them if you drop them.'

'I think I'm getting the hang…' She didn't finish. Couldn't finish because his hands were in no place to catch any falling citrus fruit. They had circled her waist and he was turning her round.

As she completed the turn she stared straight into those black pupils glittering with need. The air stilled around them, heavy with intent, like his eyes. '*God*, Lola…'

'Yes?' But she didn't hear his answer, if indeed he answered at all, because his mouth was on hers, hard and hungry. This wasn't the kind of kiss they'd shared before. This wasn't gentle or coaxing; this was pure, raw need. And she kissed him back just as hard, the oranges spinning across the floor as she dropped them to spike her fingers into his hair, to pull him closer, and ever closer.

* * *

There was only so much a guy could resist.

He'd thought earlier he was a damned saint for walking away from her—*twice*. But now he was going to hell and he outright didn't care.

Because having Lola Bennett was the only thing he'd had on his mind all damned day. All damned week, if he was honest, and if he didn't act on this he was going to implode. A mist clouded his brain as he pulled her harder to him. All he could see was Lola, all he could breathe, smell, taste was her. Nothing else mattered. Just this. And her. She mattered.

He felt her curves beneath his hands, spoke against her lips. 'Forget what I said earlier. I was an idiot. I want you, Lola. I want you, right here.'

'Finally. You know, I was starting to get a complex. One minute you wanted me, the next…not so much.'

'I always wanted you. I was trying to protect you.'

He felt her body stiffen. She took a step back. 'Whoa, mister, I don't need protecting. I'm very grateful for everything you've done for me today, but I can manage my life just fine on my own.'

'Hmm—I know, but you can't kiss on your own.' He licked behind her ear, felt her soften a little. 'Can't do this on your own. Right?'

'Good point.' She giggled—a throaty, dirty sound that stoked even more fury through his veins. Her hands were on his T-shirt, dragging it up over his head. 'Your bedroom? Or mine?'

'Not sure we'll make it that far. Next time maybe. Beds are overrated.' Right now the kitchen table looked enticing. So did the floor. He was tearing at her clothes, nipping along her throat, en route to tasting those exquisite breasts again. Luckily she still had the bikini on underneath her T-shirt and shorts—two quick tugs and she'd be naked.

Her hand stilled on his. 'Are you sure about this, Jake. I mean, really sure?'

'Do you have to ask?'

'Ya think? With your track record? I'm not going to start something if you're just going to stop and leave me frustrated. I'm over that.'

'Come with me. Now.' There weren't words enough to tell her how sure he was. He slipped his hands under her legs and picked her up, carried her to the closest soft horizontal surface he could find. One of the couches in the lounge. The flickering torchlight filtered through the blinds, illuminating her full beauty. God, she was more beautiful than a hundred Hollywood actresses. More real. Just more. So much more.

Careful of her leg, he straddled her and slammed his mouth over hers, drank her in, fed on her kisses like a starving man. Her skin was soft, her kisses hot, her moans like licks of heat piercing him. There was nothing he could do to stop this. Nothing he wanted to do more.

She raked her hands across his chest, ran her fingers over his belly towards his belt. He grabbed her hand. 'Not so fast. I want to taste you first…'

She started to undo the buckle. 'But—'

His grip tightened. 'Look here, Miss Independent…relax. Let me do something for you.'

'You've done that all day, looked after me. Now it's your turn. I want to show you my gratitude.'

'Lola,' he growled in her ear. 'I get that you want to be your own woman—but this? This is about the two of us. I want to make you feel so damned good. You first…'

She pouted and pretended to think about that

option for all of a nanosecond. Then she laughed. 'Oh, okay…if you insist.'

'I do.' His mouth was on her throat, making a soft trail to her breasts. He flicked off her bikini and sucked a nipple into his mouth. Underneath him she bucked against his hardness, a soft purr coming from her throat. Her hands fisted his hair, yanking with every lick on her nipple. 'You taste so good.'

Then things got serious as he made a slow trail down her belly, slipped off her shorts and bikini bottom. 'You have no idea how you make me feel, Lola.'

'Oh, I can guess. I feel it too.' Her palm covered him over his pants and he gasped, desperate for her to free him from the restrictive fabric. But he'd have to wait.

She gave him a slow sexy smile that glittered in her eyes, the connection deepening, the connection very real. Tangible. A fist round his heart. Damn, but he'd never felt like this about a woman before—as if there'd been something he hadn't known he'd been looking for, and now he'd found it. Like finding the last piece in a jigsaw puzzle. Complete.

And it should have scared him. Hell, it did, more than anything. He'd been fine before he'd met her—he'd already felt complete, goddammit. He didn't need a woman to make him more whole…but it also spurred him on.

He nudged her thighs apart and dipped his head, tasting the hot slickness of her as she rocked against him, her moan intensifying, urging him on. She was so wet as he stroked his tongue across that tight nub of flesh, as he gripped her backside and trapped her in place. He could sense her orgasm mounting with the tightened grasp, the sob of delight. Each moan of hers elicited a groan from him. God, he needed to be inside her.

When she shuddered he thought he might explode. When she called out his name he thought he'd die.

But she was pulling him up, reaching for his zip, pushing down his shorts, finally freeing him from all constraints. He had to be inside her. To feel her around him, to feel her climax against him. 'Condom…'

'Yes. Yes. Yes.'

He reached down to his shorts, pulled out the packet, sheathed in record time. And then she was taking control, wrapping her hand around his thickness, making him gasp.

He looked down the length of her, saw the redness of her leg… 'Wait…I don't want to hurt you.'

She gave him a smile that almost broke his heart in two. 'It's okay. You won't hurt me. I promise. Jake… I want you so much. I want you.'

He reached and bent her leg slowly so there'd be no danger of hurting her. Then she was pulling him into her, deep into her core, the silky softness wrapping around him, her muscles gripping him in a sweet tightness. His mouth covered hers in a desperate kiss, his gaze never leaving hers—the truth spinning between them, faster, mesmerising, intoxicating. If there was a heaven, this was it.

She rocked with his rhythm, urging him harder, faster, calling his name until he could take no more. Pleasure, need and hunger slammed into him, and he groaned out her name, caught the first shudders of her release. Felt the thin ethereal threads that connected them tighten. Then and only then did he finally let go.

CHAPTER NINE

WHAT THE HELL had just happened?

Lola wasn't just thinking about the sex—she was thinking about the sharp tug on her heart as she'd kissed him, eyes open, and had seen deep into his gaze. The way he'd encouraged her to be herself—to let go, to let him show her the way. Mirrored in his eyes were the emotions she'd felt, heart full, overwhelming. This wasn't just about her, this was about the two of them. Together.

Tears pricked her eyes but she blinked them away. She was surely just being silly. She couldn't feel so much for Jake after such a short time. It was dangerous, and bordering on absurd.

But she did feel something…something new.

He twisted to the side and wrapped her close in his arms, spooning behind her. And it felt right. Two hearts catching the same rhythm, breaths gradually slowing after exercise, his warmth. And he fitted around her as if he was meant to be there. So right, so crazy. Her head was spinning while he was whispering in her ear, 'See… babe magnet.'

'Believe me, this has got nothing to do with juggling oranges.'

'That's what you think.'

'I know so…' She turned and prodded his tummy as he laughed, thinking how easy it could be to relax into this and be happy. *Happy.* Now, there was a thought.

He kissed behind her ear and growled, 'It's just animal magnetism, then.'

'Yes. Probably.' And a whole lot more she didn't want to put a name to. However, it was fine to get all romantic here when neither of them had much to do. But back at work, back in Los Angeles it would be different. Busy lives. Plans. Not plans that blended easily, if at all.

Suddenly there was a warm, wet raspy feeling on her toe. 'Ugh. What the hell—? *Butter?* Oh, my God, I'd forgotten about the dogs. Look at us here, like this. Naked!' She threw back her head and laughed, because, yes, it was absurd. 'They're going to need therapy after this. We might have scarred them for life.'

Jake grabbed a throw and wrapped it around her, while he found a cushion and covered himself. And laughed, heartily. 'Shoo. Go away. No harm done. Just teaching them a thing or two. Birds and bees…or whatever it is in puppy language.'

'Thank God they can't talk.'

Butter stopped licking and twitched to the right, nose in the air, ears back. Then she began to bark. Just as the doorbell rang. A creeping panic built in Lola's chest. 'Oh…oh, could it be Cameron? Oh, hell. Quick. Clothes. On.'

'Damn. Damn. Damn.' Cushion still firmly in place, Jake jumped back then started to drag on his shorts. In her mind-melted state she did manage to sneak a look at his perfect body one last time and remember how good it had been to have the weight of him over her.

And then she gave in to her panic. The doorbell rang again. Jake offered her his hand and pulled her from the sofa, tightened the throw around her. 'Go put something on, I'll get the door. Thank God for blinds is all I can say.' He gave her the gentlest smile she'd seen in years. 'Come on, Lola. Laugh.'

She tried to smile, tried to find this the funniest thing she'd experienced in years, she did. Taking time out of work for great sex in the dining room of her boss's rented house, while looking after three dogs and nursing a sore foot. But how could she? None of this was funny. Not any more. She hissed, 'It's my job at risk. Okay? And yours possibly. But mostly mine.'

'Go. Disappear. I'll fix this.' And he wafted his hand towards her bedroom.

While in there she heard voices, one female, some thumping, a groan. It didn't sound like Cameron's vapid loud, crisp voice or Tina's laconic, lyrical tones. Then the door closed. Silence.

She thought about going out to see what was going on, but with her luck there'd be a troop of paparazzi there, waiting to ambush her. She could just imagine the headline: *'PA to the stars caught having sofa sex with a canine audience'*. Just great.

Within seconds Jake stood in her doorway, looking very pleased with himself. 'Hey, it was just Evelyn Rice, dropping off the clothes. I told her I'd just been to the beach and to excuse the clothing. She was fine. A little nosy perhaps…

she wanted to come in and meet Cameron…but just fine. She's gone, the coast is clear. Although, as we are renting this place, you have every right to be naked or otherwise.'

Having managed to shrug on a bathrobe, she followed him into the lounge and to a rack of exquisite tailored clothes in jewel colours. 'Good. Thanks. Wow, she'll love these. You arranged for her to bring them here rather than to the house?'

'I wasn't sure what to do. I thought if she brought them here I'd save face if I'd got the wrong things, Cameron need never know.'

Lola ran her hand along the rack and picked out a vivid aquamarine dress that she just knew would fit her perfectly. 'Oh, these are gorgeous. You did well. I should thank you again for arranging it all.' Yet another reminder that she was failing somewhat in her duties. Jake had taken her mind off her job, snorkelling had taken her finger off the pulse… What had she been thinking, letting him convince her to take time off? And now…sex. Sex when she was supposed to be working. 'Seems I'm all about thanking you today.'

'Hey! What's with the mood slip? Everything's

fine—no one knows what we were doing. Peanut, Butter and Jelly don't speak human, so you don't have to worry about them. Come here.' He slipped his arms around her waist and nuzzled her neck. Punctuating his words with kisses, he said, 'Stop. Worrying. It's. Going. To. Be. Fine.'

Only a few moments ago she'd thought about being happy, but now that was fading fast. She whirled round to face him, regretting having to do this but doing it anyway. There. The first regret. 'How can you be so sure everything's going to be okay?'

'Go with it, Lola. We have two more nights here—look around you, it's amazing. It's a gift.'

'We took our foot off the pedal. It could have been Cameron, Alfredo…Tina. We could have got the sack.'

'I doubt anything that dramatic would have happened. Anyway, I don't care what anyone thinks.'

'I do.' She drew away from him, her mind reeling with questions and reasons, but her body craving his touch regardless. 'Look, I don't know what to say…to think…' She cast her eyes towards the sofa where it had all happened. 'But we can't do this here.'

'No, you're right—too uncomfortable. We have two bedrooms to choose from…'

'No. I mean we can't do this. This…' In an attempt to make things clearer she wafted her hand between the two of them. Her heart had started to ache just a little at what she was about to let go. *'This.'*

Taking her wrist, he pulled her to him. 'Lola, we can do anything we damned well like.'

'Not if it means losing my job.'

His jovial smile faltered. 'Hell, you're as bad as me, work obsessed.'

Irritation started to prickle up her spine. 'Maybe, but I am also food obsessed. Rent obsessed. Paying the bills obsessed…I need this job, it was hard to come by. You try finding a job that pays enough to let you live in LA and brings you a step closer to the life you want to live.' She pushed a finger into his chest, ignoring the heat, ignoring the fading light in his eyes. 'This is my life. We don't get to jeopardise that just for a bit of sex.'

It was more than that, so much more…but how could she do this with him and keep all the promises to herself? She was here to work, to achieve her potential. Losing sight of that would be costly on so many levels.

'Okay, then how about a *lot* of sex? No?'

'You don't get it, Jake. There's too much at stake.'

'What? Exactly? Other than a job you're not fond of?'

Me. My life. My dreams. Everything I'm working for. My parents' hearts. Before she could stop him his lips melded with hers in a long slow, bone-melting kiss. She wanted to push away, to run, to shout, to make him listen to all the objections she had on her list. But he anchored her there, to him, making her feel dizzy with desire. Heat slammed into her and despite everything she wrapped her arms around his neck, not listening to the little voice in her head telling her to stop.

He was still shirtless and his naked chest was a delight to her senses—smooth skin, the solid planes of his body, the strong beat of his heart. He kissed her and kissed her some more, long and slow as if they had all the time in the world. He explored her mouth, her neck, her throat all over again. Then feasted some more on her mouth until she was weak with need, until there was nothing more she could ever want than to be here, with him.

When he finally pulled away, his smile was confident and sure—very unlike how she was feeling. 'That seems to work. Good.'

A little dizzy at the heady rush of his touch she made a bit of space between them. 'Charming.'

'I try my best.' His fingers ran down her cheek. 'I like you, Lola. In fact, to be truthful, I've never met anyone like you before. You're unique, beautiful, sexy and smart. I like who you are and what you're trying to do with your life—I totally respect that and I'm not going to get in the way of anything you want to do. A few hours ago you wanted this as much as I do. Look, I promise not to interfere with your work tomorrow or any day after that. I will be professional to the core and when we get back to LA I promise I'll dip out of your life just as you want. But right now we have something good going, and I don't see anyone holding a gun to your head and making you fill in a time sheet.'

'But—I don't know...' What the hell could she say to that? She was discombobulated by him. His kisses made her feel dizzy and stopped any kind of rational thought process—but he was only suggesting a little play. She could do that. Hell, Cameron spent most of her life playing…

His hand smoothed across the nape of her neck. 'There's not much of today left. Tomorrow we're booked up all day at the set and then the wrap dinner. That leaves us a few hours now…private and personal hours where we can do what the hell we like. I've seen plenty of Nassau, but no-where near enough of your bedroom. Now, you can either give me a sightseeing tour or I can go to bed on my own. Personally, I think that would be a big mistake.'

Lola didn't like making mistakes. Plus, he was the sexiest man she'd ever seen. What a waste if she walked away from that, from crazy commit-ment-free fun in paradise.

As he drew her closer Lola decided not to think any more. She wasn't going to ruin it by worry-ing, she was going to go with her gut. So she let him lead her into the bedroom and lay her down, relished the press of his heat and the safety of liv-ing in the moment with no regard for what tomor-row would bring.

* * *

'Hey, Jake! Dr Jake, come talk to Alfredo. He's got a problem with his gall bladder. Needs advice.' Cameron Fontaine was nothing but enthusiastic about using all Jake's talents when she wanted to; she just also dodged any direct questioning or personal one-to-one conversations.

The day had started with her personally checking up on Lola and insisting on hearing a rundown of the jellyfish barb removal all over again, in full detail. Then interspersing scene takes with chatter about healthy eating—he'd guessed that was for her own benefit, though. She'd asked pointed questions without referring to herself or a pregnancy or maternal diet. And damn if she kept herself surrounded by people.

The crowded tapas bar overlooked a marina and some of the cast and crew spilled out dockside, a few of them sitting out on one of the launches. Alfredo and Cameron were waving and shouting to them. He sauntered over. 'Alfredo, Cameron.'

'Honey, I'm going to join those reprobates over there for a little cruise around the harbour. Alfredo needs you for one second, then he's coming with me.' Cameron gave him an air kiss. 'Tell

Lola I'll need a call at five. Be good, you two. Sleep well.'

Not so fast. He followed her a step or two and tried to get her attention. 'Cameron, I need to talk with you, privately. Now.'

He doubted anyone had spoken to her like that before. Her smile faltered as she pressed her palm on her belly over her floaty dress, her voice low. 'Yes, honey, I know you know… But not here, or now—too many spies. Later, tomorrow… No, we're travelling. Wednesday? I'm back on set on Wednesday. Yes, Wednesday in my trailer.'

'Now works better for me.'

'No can do. Got to keep on top of things here. I have a boat to catch. It's worked out just fine, though? Yes? Our little secret?' With a grand flourish she gave him a second chaste air kiss. *'Ciao.'*

Jake really preferred it when he had his patients safely in the clinic environment, they were a lot less likely to run out on him—and he could at least get a word in.

Oblivious to the celebrity gossip story of the year playing out under his nose, Alfredo caught him up and shook his hand. 'Jake, I do not want to spoil your night with my medical issues—besides, business is finished for the day. But I would like to say how impressed I've been with you. An inside view on how anti-gravity affects the brain was terrific for us to play up the confusion, ramp up the effects and the emotion today. Just great. And the way you dealt with that arm injury was very impressive. Who'd have thought you could make a splint out of a rolled-up pair of trousers? Tell James I'll be sure to recommend the clinic, and specifically you, to anyone who needs a medic.'

'Thank you. James will be pleased.' Jake wasn't sure he was. If he'd been in any doubt at all, he was now convinced he didn't want to be a film medic or a secret obstetrician. He wanted to be a neurosurgeon and left in peace to get on with it. Although he had to admit he'd enjoyed today, interspersed as it had been with minor emergencies anyone with a small amount of first-aid knowledge could have dealt with. And at least Alfredo and the rest of the crew were normal human beings, even if Cameron was in a league of her own.

Mostly, he'd enjoyed last night and this morning…waking up with Lola. That had been a revelation.

The aging director gave a weary sigh. 'I'd better go join our leading lady… Wish me luck.'

'You're going to need it. Oh—and if you do need a decent gastro surgeon, just ask. I can make a few calls.'

And now what? Jake turned to see Lola sitting at a table with the location production assistant and a couple from Set Dec. They were laughing at something she was saying, her russet hair highlighted in the subdued lighting, her creamy skin illuminated and clear.

But for him nothing was clear at all—his head was awash with fresh memories of her curves, her kisses, her soft moans. Cameron had given her the pick of the Evelyn Rice dresses and she'd chosen a silk blue one that elevated her to the star of tonight's dinner. Hell, he was surrounded by Hollywood royalty and he didn't care. In fact, he was supposed to be working and his mind was not on his job. Which was, what? First time ever?

So he was in trouble and he didn't know what the hell to do about it.

He waited a few beats as the storm inside him died down, then strolled over. 'Hey.'

'Hi, Doc. We were just about to leave. Early flight and all that…' Lola smiled and stood, her eyes fixing on his. Memories of last night, of her body and what was underneath that dress intensified and reverberated between them, and he wished the rest of the crew would just disappear and leave them alone.

'Cameron's gone on a harbour cruise, she won't be back for a while. Fancy a walk back to the lodge? We could go along the beach.'

'Okay, yes. Why not?' She said her goodbyes to the team and they headed outside. The rhythmic lapping of waves soothed them into a silence as they made their way down the wooden steps to the beach.

He steadied her as she took her shoes off. 'Be careful with that ankle.'

'I'm fine, really. The hydrocortisone ointment helped a lot. I haven't felt like I wanted to scratch the whole limb off for a good few hours now.'

'That's good. I'm not sure how you'd manage walking three tearaway dogs with one leg.'

'Oh, I'd manage.'

'Sure you would.' He slipped an arm around her shoulder and they walked along slowly, sinking into the soft white sand with every step. 'Good day?'

'Oh, yes. I caught up on everything I needed to do. Thank goodness.' Her hand snaked round his waist and she slid it into the back pocket of his shorts, then rested her head against his shoulder. The air was fresh and clean and it felt good to just be out in the elements, talking about something and nothing with Lola. He couldn't remember the last time he'd done that with a woman. He couldn't remember the last woman to enthral him so much—but there was something he was missing. A piece of that jigsaw that had come unstuck. Judging by her extreme reaction to almost being caught having sex, there was more to Lola's story, but she was keeping tight-lipped about it.

She smiled up at him. 'So, Cameron did just fine with the dream scenes, don't you think?'

'Sure.' He hadn't noticed. 'How much filming is left?'

'Once we get back there're some night shoots, then it moves into post-production and we move on. Cameron's got a month or so before she starts rehearsals for her next film, which is a big cow-boy saga.'

'Involving horse-riding, I imagine?' Jake huffed out a breath. At some point the woman was going to have to embrace it and announce her pregnancy, and then the correct safety measures could be put in place for her. Again, no issues with horse-riding in pregnancy, but that kind of activity carried a risk and she needed to know what it was. And so did her co-stars and director.

Lola smiled. 'Yes. Why?'

'No reason. Just wondering. One day it's space, the next it's the Wild West...I don't know how you do it.'

'It's exciting. No two days are the same.' Lola's smile distracted him from his work thoughts. 'Glad you're leaving all this madness soon?'

'Yes. And no. I have a full clinic the day after we get back and surgery booked the day after that, and I have to fit visits to the set in between times. Night shoots will work well and shouldn't disrupt anything at the clinic. Who needs sleep?'

'See? You're getting into the swing of this life.' She gave him a little nudge in the ribs with her elbow, her voice soft. 'But tomorrow we're back to reality.'

'We always knew it would happen.'

'Yes. I just didn't expect...' She came to a stop and gazed out at the ocean. A bright moon lit up the surface and he remembered swimming with the dolphins. The ocean kiss. The way he'd tried, and failed, to keep away from her—for what? Looking back, being with her had been inevitable. She sounded wistful. 'I didn't expect for so much to happen here.'

His chest suddenly tightened. 'You could always come back some time.'

'It wouldn't be the same.' She turned and gave him a knowing look—and, yes, he was expert at avoiding intimate conversation, but they both knew what this was, and what it wasn't. Neither of them needed a complication in their real lives. 'These things never are, are they? A good rule is to never go back to a place if you've had the best fun there—you're just chasing a dream and it's never as good the second time round. Having said that, my mum would love it here. It's exactly what she needs. City life is all very well, but this is so peaceful everyone should come here once in their lives. I'm going to email her about it. Maybe she could bring my sister and I could meet them here. Family vacation.'

'You're close? You and your sister? You've never mentioned her.'

'Oh, you know, as close as you can be when you live thousands of miles apart. She's three years older than me, a teacher, like my dad. We're just a regular two-point-four family.'

He wondered what that felt like. There'd been so much pressure on him as an only child. He'd been everything in his parents' lives. At times it had been too much and he'd become so frustrated that they'd poured all their hopes and dreams into him.

The guilt started to bite.

'Yeah. Dad would love it here too.' He tried not to give in to the familiar spiral of bleakness at the thought of his father. The tight clench of his gut was visceral and instinctive. He breathed in deeply again… It seemed tonight was all about the sharp clutch in his chest and the sinking feeling in his belly whichever way he turned.

Lola linked her arm through his with a breezy smile. 'Then make it happen. Bring them. We could have a family reunion. Actually, no. Forget I said that. It would be weird. But bring them. A holiday of a lifetime.'

'It wouldn't be the same.' He kissed her neck, hoping she understood what he meant without putting his heart on his sleeve. If she hadn't been here it would have been a very dull…what had she called it? A very dull *jolly*. 'Dad's not great at going on vacation.'

'Like his son?'

'This is hardly a vacation. And…'

She nudged him to continue. 'And what?'

'Ah, nothing.' This was private stuff…something he didn't usually share with other people.

'Something, I think, or you wouldn't have gone all quiet and moody. Talk to me, Jake. It's our last night here.'

'And spoil it with my stuff? I don't think so.'

She stared out at the ocean again. 'All that out there, so vast and wide… And all this in here…' She prodded his chest. 'All caught up in a tight ball of hurt. Whatever it is, let it go.'

'Are those drugs still affecting your brain?' He tried to laugh, but it didn't come out right. And she was here and, well, hell…*she was here*, and something about that made it easier for him to think and to speak. He followed her gaze out to sea. 'He's sick, Lola. Very. He can't travel far, he needs oxygen to help him breathe. It's hard to travel with a tank by your side, and wheelchair access is terrible everywhere—his excuse, not mine. I keep telling him nothing's impossible, but he doesn't listen. That's half his problem. He's a stubborn old coot.'

'That's where you get it from, then.' Holding his hand tightly, she tugged him to sit down on the sand with her. 'I'm sorry he's sick, Jake.'

And the guilt rolled and rolled through him. 'I'm trying to get him the best treatment, arranged plenty of appointments, but he won't come to the city—says he has everything he needs in Van Nuys. He's used to the doctors there and likes his home comforts. I know he could do better with my colleagues. He just won't listen.' He was going to die and everything Jake had been trying to do would be futile.

She stroked down his back. 'What's wrong with him?'

'COPD. Chronic obstructive pulmonary disease. He's a chronic asthmatic, and a few years ago he got a serious lung infection too. He was really sick, but the stubborn old goat didn't get help until it was almost too late.'

'That must have been scary for you all.'

Jake's chest was sore as he remembered the phone call at med school. His mother's shaking voice. The plummeting of his gut. His father on life support. *He was like that because of me.*

'He'd been working two jobs to pay my college fees. Said a good father wouldn't see his son facing huge bills, so instead of going to the doctor he carried on working. My mom worked shifts back then, so she didn't see him much and didn't realise how sick he was getting. He nearly didn't make it. Since then things haven't improved much. His lungs are fragile and vulnerable to infection. He had to give up those two jobs, now he's housebound, depressed and cantankerous with not much left to look forward to. Mom gave up work to care for him.'

'And you think it's your fault?'

'He did all that for me, pressed on for me, worked himself too hard for me. There's a common denominator there and it's got my name on it. Wouldn't you feel guilty?'

'Oh, yes.' She leaned her head on his shoulder. 'I know why you would, believe me.'

'Why?'

She waved her hand, blinking fast. 'Oh…I just imagine I would too. I can see why you'd want to help, to fix it. But he chose to do those things, Jake. He chooses not to get the right help. And sometimes you just can't fix everything.'

Guilt turned into frustration and he edged away from her, wanting some space. She didn't need this stuff in her life. 'I've paid him back, every cent. Doubled. I send them cash every month for bills, for anything they need, but it just accumulates in a bank account they won't touch. He won't accept my help. Says it's a father's work to help out a son and not the other way round. He's too darned proud.'

'And you try to pay him back by working just as hard as he did? Harder? Now I understand why you're so dedicated, so driven. It's not about the job, it's about your dad. About being good enough, about being worth the sacrifice? If you're so fixed on him getting the money back, go and see him and try to convince him to take it, face-to-face.'

The weight of it all hung heavily on his shoulders. 'You think I haven't? Over and over again until I just gave up trying. He won't take it. If he did he'd believe he'd failed as a parent, as a man.'

Her eyes never left his as she shook her head. 'Then just go see him and talk, Jake. Tell him that you love him, that you're grateful for what he did—not angry. No pressure, no money talk. Just see him. That's all he'll want. To know that you've turned out to be a good man—that everything he did was worth it. Put the anger aside and give him your gratitude. Tell him how you feel.'

'He knows how I feel.'

'Are you sure? I'm no expert—really, I don't do family dynamics well. But dig deeper, Jake.'

'It's not as if I haven't tried, Lola. But every damned time I go I get so angry with them we have an argument. I know he could be better cared for, I know he could have a better life and I can't watch him waste away when I can help.' He heard the reactive anger in his voice and tried to dampen it, but failed. And if he looked closely inside himself, Jake knew those visits were diffi-

cult because of things *he* said and felt, not neces-
sarily his parents. The sad truth was, it was easier
to bury himself in work than it was to try to fix
things back at home.

Not wanting to talk about that any more, he
turned to her. 'When we go back—'

'No. Don't talk about going back,' Lola interrupted in a whisper, and reached for him. 'Don't
talk about what's going to happen.'

'Things will change.'

'Hush. Don't break the spell.' She circled her
arms around his neck and pulled him to lie with
her. The white sand was soft beneath his body,
a warm breeze floated over them and for many
moments he just looked at her and marvelled at
how one person could soothe away the anger. She
had a way of seeing inside him, of looking for the
good in him and making that good come out, no
problem at all. She made smoothing over things
with his family seem possible. Within reach.

She traced her finger over his lips. 'Can you
hear the waves? Can you see that sky? A million
stars. A billion.' She laughed. 'A billion trillion.
Oh, I don't know, I'm no good at maths.

'Let's celebrate that, Jake. Let's not allow anyone or anything to spoil tonight. Reality's for tomorrow. Okay? I want you. Let's make right now perfect.'

The kiss she gave him was more than he deserved, more than he could ever have imagined. Sweet, slow and giving until the frustration and the anger and all thoughts of his father and the differences between Lola and himself drifted away.

It was a long time before she let go, but when she did there was renewed heat in her eyes. She wanted him. Here. The glittering in her eyes was golden, rich and warm. And the current in the air seemed to be supercharged with need. She reached for his shirt buttons and began to slip them open.

And there was no more talking as he bent to kiss her again. He slipped his hand underneath her top and started to explore the curves and dips that he had come to know so well in such a short space of time. They had all night on a deserted beach underneath a canopy of stars in a midnight sky. She wanted perfection, and he aimed to give her exactly that. Before she started talking time sheets again and before he dipped out of her life. Like he'd promised to do.

Sometimes promises came at a cost. He just hadn't expected this one to be so high.

CHAPTER TEN

LOLA WOKE WITH a start. Shards of yellow moonlight filtered through the white wooden slats, casting Jake's room in a warm liquid honey glow. Which was exactly what she'd felt falling asleep in his arms.

Even now he slept with an arm draped over her, possessive, keeping her close. And she liked that—liked that he seemed to crave her touch as much as she craved his. A strange feeling, this. A need like she'd never had before.

His breath whispered along her neck, his lithe, toned body totally relaxed in sleep. His face was inches from hers and she looked at him, committing the enviably long eyelashes, the tiny bump along his nose and his proud jawline to memory.

Because they hadn't discussed the *What next?* step and she was all kinds of confused about what she wanted now. What should she do for the best—for *her* best? If she committed herself to Jake, wouldn't she be doing exactly what she'd sworn not to do—be responsible for someone else's happiness? And yet the thought of a Jake-free life had her stomach spiralling into freefall.

The alarm began its shrill cacophony and as she reached to hit the snooze button the dogs began to bark. She collapsed back onto the pillow, laughing. 'Oh, yes. Wakey-wakey, world. No rest for the wicked.'

'We weren't all that wicked, Lola. Just a little bit. In fact…now I think about it, not nearly wicked enough.' Jake's arm tightened around her waist, preventing her from getting out of bed. 'We've only just closed our eyes. What time is it?'

'Four-thirty.'

'The middle of the night? What the hell?'

She gave him a quick kiss on his mussed-up hair, a lump tight in her throat. 'Someone's grumpy today.'

'Today? It's still yesterday as far as I'm concerned. It's not today until either the sun comes up, or I've had at least five hours' sleep.' Something hard prodded her thigh and she grinned. His voice was husky with sleep and desire. 'Do you know what would make me feel a whole lot better?'

Damn right, it would make her feel better too. So would spending the rest of the day here. But it was impossible—real life was back with a vengeance.

'Nothing would get my day off to a better start, believe me, but we have to get going. We should have packed last night instead of...' Like hell she'd have preferred packing to making love on a beach. Or showering the sand off later, together... Her body thrummed with the soft ache of exercise, and she had an inner glow that would keep her warm for some time to come, but that didn't stop time marching on. Too quickly. 'I'm sorry, Jake. Come on. Time to get up. The fun's over.'

'Why?'

'We're going home. We talked... It's over.'

'Whoa. Wait a minute. What's the hurry?' He sat up. His hand closed over hers and made her pause as her heart began to pump against her ribcage. 'What do you mean?'

'We have a plane to catch.'

'Yes, and we're ahead of schedule. So why are you running?'

'I'm not running.'

'Could have fooled me.' He tugged on her hand. 'Look at me, Lola. Look at me.'

It all suddenly seemed too hard. She didn't want a sad goodbye, she just wanted to leave without pain. She started to throw her clothes into her bag. 'I have too much to do. This isn't the time or place, Jake.'

'You think? I have a few questions for you…so hear me out. What is this rush? Why is pleasing Cameron so important to you? I mean, really? Why? It's like it's the biggest thing in your life. It's not even the job you want.'

'It's not about the job.' She wasn't going to discuss it here. 'Come on, let's get packed or you'll make us late.'

'And that would never do, right?' He grabbed the pillow and pulled it onto his head. 'I'm not moving, Lola. Not until you tell me what the hell is going on.'

'You'd do that? You'd make things worse for me?'

'If it meant I got the truth, yes. If it's not about the job, what is it about?'

She glanced at the clock and her heart beat a

little faster. 'And now there's a time restriction on my words. Great.' But he did deserve some kind of explanation, because she had to admit her obsession with making everything work for her probably did seem a little extreme. 'Okay… well. This is the situation… And don't judge me, okay?' She twisted the sheet in her fist, screwing it tighter and tighter, because admitting this was like exposing a raw nerve. 'My family doesn't know anything about my writing. They think I'm in LA to act. It's all I've ever done since I was a baby. All they've ever wanted me to do. And I hate it. The last thing I want to do is get up on a stage and say someone else's words. I want to write my own.'

'They think you're here to…' He smiled. 'Way to go. That's why you won't send your dad the script.'

'He'd go crazy—you have no idea. They think I have *it*. You know, that little nugget of talent to be great, and they'd think I was throwing a huge opportunity away. Just like Dad did. But it's their dream, Jake, not mine. They won't listen, of course, because they want to live vicariously through me. They trussed me up and pushed me onto stages, into advertisements, pantomimes, TV shows, anything where I could *shine*. Paid for acting lessons, one-on-one tuition, immersion classes, dancing…anything I earned went straight back into my drama education. It was relentless. They pushed and pushed and pushed until I'd had a gut full of learning lines and make-up and playing nice or playing naughty or being Santa's helper or a dead body or bloody Lady Macbeth. I'd had enough, so I left. I needed to come to a place where I could be me. If they knew I wasn't even trying to act here, they'd be devastated. So I have to make this work. My script, my dream. My choice. My life. Do you see? I have to make it work and that takes dedication, time management, studying, practice—a whole lifetime of catching up. And now…look, you're making me late. I can't be late. I can't take a chance on losing this job, because, apart from giving me enough money to just about survive here, working for Cameron helps with the pretence…'

'The lie.'

'Yes.' She tilted her chin. She wasn't proud of it, but she would do anything to get where she wanted to be. Including misleading her family.

'The lie. Oh, it's easy when you have someone who wants you to follow your dreams, altogether another when they won't even let you have one of your own. Now, please. Can we go? I will tell them. I will. When I've sold my script. When I'm ready—and not when you or anyone else decides. Now we have to go. Okay?'

'Okay. Okay.' His palms went up. He was frowning. Now he knew she wasn't who she'd said she was. She was someone who would break her parents' hearts just to be free. Then he stroked the inside of her arm and made her shiver. 'I wouldn't tread on your dreams, Lola. I wouldn't jeopardise them.'

Making me fall for you would do exactly that. This was too damned hard. 'Please, hurry. Cameron will be waiting.'

The catch in her throat as she gave him one final kiss was with her as she threw her clothes into her suitcase, fed the dogs, gave them their anti-nausea medicine, took them for one last walk along that divine beach. It was still there as she wheeled the rack of clothes up to the house for collection later. And when he held the car door open for her and gave her a smile that told her he was thinking of last night, and the earlier hours of this morning, and the things they'd done and the way they'd made each other feel. And not about what she'd told him and how damned selfish she could be.

She tried to ignore the prickle of sadness that had lodged behind her ribcage, and the thickness in her throat. And she dug deep and found the joy she infused into everything—regardless of whatever came next she was happy simply because it had happened.

The flight back was less serene than the one out. Butter had eaten something that upset her and spent the journey being ill, Cameron slept with earmuffs and an eye mask, and Jake stared out of the window.

When they hit the tarmac in Los Angeles, Lola still didn't know what to say to Jake. It was all well and good when you wrote the dialogue, but not when you actually lived the big, dark conflict in the story.

And this time she was tasked with picking up Cameron's suitcases while, for once, the actress took the dogs through customs, looking like a devoted and doting dog-owner and not the rather absent one she'd been in Nassau.

So there was only a quick moment to chat to Jake as he waited for a cab to take him home. No fine limousines here—at least, not for the hired help. Lola turned to him and her heart jittered a little and her cheeks burned. She wanted to touch him, to run her hands over his face, to lay her head against his chest. To kiss him once more. But she did none of those things. She stood a little apart from him and gave him a pathetic wave. 'Okay, well, that was fun! Thanks so much! I guess I'll see you on set? Wednesday?'

'Yes. Wednesday. Lola—' He took a step forward but the cab driver tooted and Cameron was shouting and the dogs were barking again and Lola started to feel as queasy as Butter.

'Okay! I need to go!' She turned to walk away.

'Lola…wait.'

'Yes?' She whizzed round, tangling herself in the trolley wheels as the suitcases swung one way and she the other.

'Watch it!' He gave her a rueful grin. 'Listen. It's been…great.'

She tightened her grip on the trolley handle and fixed her smile. 'Yes, it has. Great.'

'So…let's just see what happens, eh?'

Which could have been Jake-speak for *Don't call me, I'll call you.* Or could have been a damned offer of marriage or something in between, she didn't know. For someone who was largely direct and open, he was being remarkably tight-lipped. But she didn't have time to ponder any more. Other people needed her. More to the point, she needed some space to think about what had happened and just exactly how she felt about it all. About him.

She reached and gave his hand a tight squeeze, which was Lola-speak for *I have no bloody idea.*

Then started on the rest of her day.

Routine was good. Routine soothed his brain. Routine erased all thoughts except the purity of surgery and healing his patients.

Jake liked routine. He was back in his space and could breathe easily.

Well, easier.

'I don't like the way that artery is leaking.' He spoke to his assistant quietly and calmly, pointing to the ooze coming from around the middle cerebral artery. Jake checked the three-dimensional computer imaging again—the mass had been completely resected and the leak was minimal. There was no desperate urgency. But there was a definite need to stop the damned thing. 'Great. You got it. Excellent.' He raised his voice a little. 'How are you doing, Moira? Won't be long now.'

Their patient's eyelids fluttered open. 'Just fine, thanks.'

'Great, can you sing me something? *Carmen* maybe? Just quietly…'

'"Habanera"?' The famous opera singer smiled as the anaesthesiologist adjusted the oxygen mask so she could inhale deeply and sing. 'Oh, yes. Of course, my favourite. I'd love to…' And so she began… *"'L'amour est un oiseau rebelle. Que nul ne peut apprivoiser…'"*

Her strong melodious voice filled the OR. He'd asked her to sing quietly, but there was nothing about this woman that was quiet. She was a joy to watch on stage and he intended to keep her up there for many more years, having removed the meningioma. A little recuperation and she'd hopefully be free from the headaches and blurred vision that she'd ignored for the last few months due to her heavy work schedule. Some people put work too far up their priority list to the detriment of everything else.

Listen to yourself.

'Just perfect. Not long now. We've got all of the tumour out and, as you can see, none of your speech or memory functions have been affected.' They were of the most concern to her—she wanted to be able to remember the words and the tunes, but mostly she wanted to remember her children, the little moments, the everyday. He started to hum the catchy refrain as they began to close up the incision. 'So, what do the words mean?'

She was sleepy, but in control. 'Love is a rebellious bird, that none can tame…'

Ain't that the truth?

Whoa. Nobody said anything about love. Three days in Nassau, that's all it had been. A little before that. Nothing since. Lola's admission had been a surprise, but it explained a lot about her drive and persistence. He just wasn't at all sure what it meant for them. Thinking they both needed space, he'd avoided calling her. He wished he hadn't, but there it was.

Routine. He stuck to his routine. Nothing in his routine involved seeing a woman for more than a few dates. 'Excellent. Philip is going to finish up while I go talk to your kids. They've been waiting outside for you. You're very loved.'

She squeezed his hand. 'I know. I'm very blessed. My children are devoted. Go, tell them I'm fine.'

He washed up and wandered out to the family room where he found Moira's son and daughter— both around his age, in their early thirties—pale with worry. He'd been there on the other side a couple of times, waiting for the prognosis on his father. He knew how they felt, the anguish, the pain. Knew how to be honest but to tread lightly. Knew that they wouldn't rest until they saw her. As he approached they both stood, stepped forward, worry smudged across their faces. 'Dr Jake…how is she? Is she okay?'

'She's fine. She's actually been great through the whole procedure. She's sedated a little, and will now be able to rest, but we'll keep a close eye on her.'

The son stepped forward and shook his hand. 'Thank you. Thank you. I don't know what we'd have done without her. She's…well, she's just the best mom.'

She was also the best mezzo-soprano in the world, but they wouldn't care as much about that as having their mother alive. 'No problem at all. I understand. I'll be back later to check up on her.'

As he strode down the corridor he felt a sharp sting in his chest. He'd hated being on the other side, hated being out of control, and had wanted anything for his father to live. He could still re-member the pain of waiting, the promises he'd made, the deals he'd forged between himself and some higher being—*if he survives I'll repay him every last cent. If he lives I'll show him it was worth it. Just let him live.* It was still raw, like a hard lump in his ribcage.

But for what? All he had done since had been to berate his father for working himself into an early grave, for not listening to his son's advice, for not letting him take on the burden. Something that Lola had said to him about showing grati-tude struck a chord. He flicked out his phone and dialled.

* * *

Five hours later, with something of a little respite in that heartburn, he arrived at the set for the night shoot. There were two things on his agenda tonight and he was going to achieve them, whatever else happened. Unfortunately they both depended on Cameron being amenable.

Not seeing her on set, he meandered over to the trailers and rapped sharply on the door to Cameron's. The loud yelping of three dogs greeted him as Lola answered. She was wearing that Evelyn Rice blue dress she'd had on the other night, her hair was piled loosely on her head, accentuating her eyes, which were back to being guarded again. He wanted to kiss that away. Actually, he wanted to make love with her again right now. But although there were very strange things happening on the space-desert-warrior-princess set, sex wasn't one of them. Even so, his body reacted to her instinctively, taking in her curves, her soft lips…

Her smile slipped as she looked at him. 'Oh. Jake. Hi.'

He wasn't sure exactly what sort of greeting it was meant to be, but it didn't say, *We had great sex, let's do it again. Soon.* Or...*I missed you.* It didn't even have the hallmarks of Lola's usual happy-go-lucky, semi-forced jolly *Hello!* complete with the requisite unspoken exclamation point. But it wasn't a damning indictment either.

He was at a loss how to navigate this. He could pretend that things hadn't changed, but they had. He knew her now—knew what she was fighting, knew how beautiful she was, knew that she was scared to take any risks that would jeopardise her plans. 'Hey, Lola. How's things?'

'Great. Thanks.'

'The leg? How's it doing?'

'Fine, thank you.' Giving nothing away, she looked down at her ankle and he followed her line of vision. It was still red and slightly swollen but he could see from this angle that things were progressing nicely. 'Oh, get down, Jelly.'

'Hey, dog.' He reached in to pat the pup, who was trying to climb up his leg, and was immediately subsumed by an intense pungent smell. Not Lola's intimate flowery scent, something altogether more pungent coming from inside the trailer. He gave her a questioning smile and whispered, 'What the hell's that smell?'

'Rosemary and geranium. Memory and stress.' There was no congenial smile, no conspiratorial grin. No joke about the strangeness of this world they were in. Instead, she took a step back up into the trailer and let him in. 'Cameron, it's Jake.'

Great, she was here. He'd have to speak to Lola later. Now he would deal with item one on his agenda: he would speak to Cameron about the pregnancy. Now. Tonight. No excuses. Work. Work. Work.

'Dr Jake, honey. Thank you for stopping by.' It was said so casually, as if he was here entirely for his own benefit and not because he was contracted to fulfil her every need. Cameron patted the sofa. 'Sit, please. I have five minutes. Let's talk.'

'Okay. Right…in that case…' Lola looked at them both, then filled the ensuing heavy silence with a scrabble around for dog leads. 'I'll take the dogs out.'

Not so fast. If she was dashing off this was probably his only chance to achieve item two on his agenda, so he had to say something before she left. With no regard for how Cameron might take this exchange he managed to attract Lola's eye and spoke to her. 'Wait, Lola. I need to talk to you too.'

'The dogs need to go out and you're here for Cameron.' With that she was gone.

And he should have been grateful for the chance to see Cameron alone, but he really wanted to chase Lola down, kidnap her and take her back to his apartment. To unwrap that dress for a second time and take her to his bed. The intensity with which he wanted her was alarming. Overwhelming. He wasn't sure at all about how he'd handled their last conversation, but what to say in a cacophony of noise and a time constraint? He stared at the space where she'd been standing and was at a loss as to what to think.

'Dr Jake?'

Work. That was what he did best. Not relationships. The disaster between him and his parents was proof enough of that. 'Cameron. Yes. Sorry. We need to talk.'

'I know we do.' The actress sat, arranged her warrior princess skirts around her and then looked directly at him. 'Yes, I am pregnant. There. I've said it. First time too. Out loud. Although my head's been in a whirl for weeks. I'm pregnant and I'm scared and I have a contract for another film starting in a month's time and I don't know what to do. There it is.'

He wanted to ask if she was happy about it, but she didn't look it. She looked young and vulnerable and terrified, and for once in her life she wasn't acting.

'How far along do you think you are? Do you know?'

'Four months or so, I guess.'

Whoa. Her waist was tiny, so either she was naturally petite or she'd been starving herself. He was concerned it was the latter, having seen how little she'd eaten in Nassau. 'First, there's nothing to be scared about, it's a perfectly natural state, but there are some considerations you could make to ensure you and the baby are in the best possible shape. Firstly, you need an OB/GYN and a midwife who can walk you through the steps. They'll give you information and advice, can book blood tests and scans, and they will put your mind completely at rest. You may have one in mind, but if not, I can refer you to one at The Hills. Gabriella Cain is excellent—'

'No.' Cameron's voice was leading-lady commanding but laced with anxiety. 'I mean, yes.

But not until this film wraps, okay? I don't want anyone to know. No one, d'you hear me?'

'I do. But Gabriella's entirely professional and will be completely confidential, and the sooner you book in to see her the better.'

'Next week, Jake. I will see her late next week once we're done here. Now, I don't want to talk about it again. Not a word until this...' she waved her hand at the trailer and nodded as if he'd already agreed and there was no more debate. '...is over. Not a word.'

'But—' The damned woman was refusing to even talk about it?

'Please...' She gave him a genuinely wobbly smile and leaned closer. 'We all have secrets, Jake. Look at you and Lola—don't deny it. It's obvious to everyone. You're not fooling anyone.'

That was none of her business. 'There is no me and Lola.'

'Whatever you say.' Surprisingly, she covered his hand with hers. 'See? Sometimes we need to hug our secrets to ourselves for a little longer until they take root. Yes? I just need to keep this secret mine before the whole world starts speculating about who the father is and what I'm going to do. And asking whether it's the death of my career. I also need to talk with my agent and the director on *Hayley's Way*, do you understand?'

He had to agree he'd wondered all of those things. 'Of course. Of course, but rest assured no one from the clinic will leak the information.'

'Honey, everyone has a price.'

'I don't.'

'No. I don't imagine you do.' Bored or weary or just plain over the conversation, he didn't know, Cameron lay back on the sofa. 'So let me wait a week longer before all hell descends—it'll be chaos and poor Lola will take most of the hits. She answers the phone, she deals with every-thing...everything. But you've been very kind so if I can do anything for you...anything you need...just ask.'

Instinct told him not to even consider a con-versation about his life or what he needed, but his mind started to work through the pros and cons and ramifications. This could be his chance to get item two on his agenda sorted. And as he worked out what to say about that another germ of an idea started to form... This could be bril-liant. Lola would probably want to kill him, but it would be brilliant. 'Actually, Cameron, there is something you could do for me...'

CHAPTER ELEVEN

'I SHOULD BE very cross with you.' Lola opened the door of her tiny Inglewood studio apartment, embarrassed that Jake would see the almost-closet she lived in, and simultaneously trying to control her erratic heartbeat. She'd received a strange call from him, asking her to be free on Saturday. No clues about why. And nothing from him since.

Now he was standing in the doorway, hair slightly damp from a recent shower, smelling fresh and clean and appetising. The grey T-shirt accentuated his toned body, the jeans underlining the casual clothes he'd told her to wear. 'You should not have asked Cameron if I could have the day off without my permission.'

'So you said on the phone. Twice. But you'd gone AWOL with the dogs, so I had no choice. In fact, the words I used to her were, "If Lola wanted the day off on Saturday, could she have it?" At that point I didn't know if you'd agree to this. Isn't everyone supposed to have two days a week off anyway?'

'In the real world, yes. In Cameron's world, not so much. Anyway…what's the big surprise?'

'You deserve a day out. I thought we could have a trip down to the beach. Then…' Jake glanced at his shoes then back at her, and she got the distinct impression he was having trouble asking her whatever it was he was asking her. 'My parents are preparing dinner for us.'

'Your what? You want me to go with you to see your parents?' *What the hell?*

Maybe 'Let's see what happens' really had been a marriage proposal? No?

No.

And in a pink polka dot sundress she was hardly dressed for a dinner with his parents.

His eyebrows rose in a question. 'Big deal?'

Yes. Huge damned deal. Especially after everything she'd told him. 'It depends. Why do you want me to go with you?'

He shrugged. 'You said I should go see them. So I'm going. This is all your fault…' When he realised that wasn't going to work he gave her a smile that he must have known would have her saying yes immediately. 'Lola, they're nice people. Besides, I thought you might like the drive out. I can show you around the area, seeing as you're new here and all.'

So basically he was acting on her advice and he wanted her to ride shotgun. 'You want support? Sure. Say the words. Ask me and I'll think about it, but don't use me as an excuse. Dr Direct has suddenly become Dr Coy—and I'm not sure how I feel about that.'

'Dr Direct? Really?'

'Yes, too direct sometimes but, yes. You say what you think. Honesty is a good thing.' She should try it herself once or twice.

'That's my philosophy too. Usually.' Actually, it was funny to see him try to ask for something. In the time she'd known him he'd been very good at giving, at anticipating, at looking after everyone, but he obviously wasn't used to asking for things for himself. That made her heart squeeze a little, but not enough that she was going to take pity on him.

'Okay. Lola, I'd like you to come and see my parents. I think we'd get along better if we had a buffer. You. This was your idea. Please.'

Her eyes narrowed. 'That was almost… Try harder next time. And I'm coming along as a what, exactly? A mysterious friend?'

'Yes. Well, not that mysterious.'

'Your friend.' It was a statement, not a question. And clearly not a proposal.

She laughed to herself, because there was a tiny part of her that had died a little. *Hope.*

She had no place hoping for something that was so out of reach for her right now.

He came over and took her into his arms. 'Aren't you? A friend?'

'I'm not sure what we are. To be honest, I don't know how to react around you.'

He frowned. 'Why not?'

'Because of what I told you the other day.'

'What I heard was that you're a young woman out living her life. Nothing wrong with that. I'm just not sure where I fit in.'

You and me both. 'Friends, like we just said. That would work.' Maybe that was enough for now. Although she had a feeling that where he was concerned she'd never have enough. That was what frightened her. 'Okay, I'd love a day out. Which beach should we go to?'

'Well, we could detour via Santa Monica. Grab some lunch, take a walk down the pier.'

'I don't know…' She grimaced. 'The last time I was at a beach I got bitten by a man-eating plant.'

'No…the last time you were on a beach something entirely different happened.' He tipped her chin up and planted a kiss on her mouth. 'Which I seem to remember you enjoyed so much you had me do it all over again in the shower…and in bed…over and over.'

With the memories of their last night on Nassau swirling in her head, she blushed. Blushed, and a hot rush of need swirled with her thoughts. 'Oh, God. Yes.'

'Later maybe?' His lips brushed hers. 'Hmm. Later definitely. But first I promise I'll look after you and protect you from the man-eating plants and aquatic life.'

'Okay, I'll just get my bag.' She turned away from him, realising, too late, that it wasn't the sea life she needed protection from. It was the damage he would do to her heart.

Lola had been to Santa Monica many times before. She loved the shopping and the relaxed beach community atmosphere, particularly down the promenade, but coming here with Jake gave it even more appeal. As usual there were street performers playing music, some dancers and a couple of jugglers wowing the crowds. Having bought the best salted caramel gelato Lola had ever tasted, they stopped for a while to lick the drips from their fingers and watch the entertainment.

As one of the jugglers threw three lit fire sticks into the air she nudged Jake. 'There you go. If ever brains turn out not to be your thing, there's always a place for you here.'

He laughed. 'Well, it would be nice to work outdoors every now and then.'

'And there's balls, sticks *and* hoops—a lot of diversity in the role.'

'Probably wouldn't pay as well as my current job.'

'But look at the smiling faces.'

His eyebrows rose. 'Hey, I make people smile. Sometimes, if I'm not careful it's a wonky smile… but still…' He grabbed her arm. 'Come on, let's hit the pier.'

You make me *smile*, she thought, and then tried

not to think and just live in the moment. Because she didn't get many moments like this, when she wasn't worrying or working. Usually both at the same time.

The afternoon flew by in a whirl of laughter. Joining the crowds of tourists, he dragged her onto the Ferris wheel and pointed out important landmarks, they swam in the sea and she pretended all over again to be attacked by a killer plant just so he could rescue her. They ate freshly baked pretzels from a stall and he tried—and failed—to get her onto the roller coaster. She was keen to walk and swim and enjoyed the carousel, but turning her upside down might have made the pretzel reappear. and she wasn't sure he'd be impressed by that.

Just as they were making their way back to the car his phone rang.

'My mom,' he explained, looking at the small screen. 'I'll just take this. Hang on.'

As he stepped away from her Lola watched his whole demeanour change. There was no smile now. His shoulders had started to hunch and his jaw clenched as he gripped the phone. His voice rose. 'No. No, Mom, that's not okay…' He paused to listen. Then, 'I don't care. I want them to take him to The Hills, to my clinic. For God's sake, Mom, he'll be seen immediately, he'll be looked after better. This time I'm not taking no for an answer, okay?'

Lola laid her hand on a taut shoulder and smoothed a palm down his back. Jake turned and gave her a weary shrug, shaking his head at the phone with irritation. 'Mom. Listen to me… Okay, put them on. Hi, it's Dr Lewis here, yes, I'm his son. Yes, I know his condition. Absolutely not. Take him to The Hollywood Hills Clinic, I can get him seen much quicker. I'll meet you there.'

He slid the phone into his pocket and stood there, taking several deep breaths.

'Your dad?'

'Turns out even the thought of seeing me gets him worked up. His breathing's off, his oxygen sats are down. They're taking him—' He exhaled his irritation as he started to pace up and down. 'Why did I say we'd go for dinner? I know he gets stressed just at the thought of me. I shouldn't have arranged anything.'

Lola knew what a burden it was to be the absolute focus of someone else's hopes; that it felt as if you carried sole responsibility for a parent's happiness—and in Jake's case their health too. She also knew that at some point you had to unshackle yourself from that, to stop taking the blame for their problems. 'This is not your fault, Jake.'

The look he gave her was bleak as they marched towards the car. 'Well, it sure as hell isn't anyone else's.'

'How's he doing?' Jake dashed into the HDU and found his mom, pale and red-eyed, by the side of the large bed. Her fingers absentmindedly worried the handles of her worn-out bag. She was dressed in a shabby beige coat he remembered she'd been excited about buying years ago. Her shoes were scuffed and a little battered. Like her heart. Looking after an obstinate old fool who preferred to eke out a tired life than take a handout from his son had worn her away at the edges.

Anger rose in his gut. His dad might have been too proud, but his mother could have had her pick of anything in Macy's. She'd have liked that, he was sure.

And, hell, that was not what was important right now.

'He's a lot better than he was. He got really out of breath and worked up—he's been in a lousy mood all day. He went a little blue and I was… well, let's just say I'm grateful we're here. The nebulisers are definitely working and it's a really nice place. Thank you, Jake… Oh!' His mom looked surprised to see Lola behind him. Why the hell he'd asked his mom to cook them dinner he didn't know. It had seemed like a good idea at the time. He'd never mentioned the word 'date', of course, but his mother's head would be working overtime, trying to join dots that didn't exist. 'Hello, you must be…?'

'Lola.' She stepped forward with a smile and gave his mom's hand a shake. 'I hope it's okay for me to be here? Jake said—'

'It's fine for you to be here.' He grabbed her a chair and had her sit next to his mom. 'This is my mom, Deanna, and my dad, Bill.'

His father lay propped up by pillows, his breath rattling in and out, with an oxygen mask over his face. His cheeks were dark hollows, his eyes scared and piercing. He'd lost more weight, Jake noticed. Constantly fighting for air did that to a man.

Jake laced his voice with as much positivity as he could muster. 'Hey, Dad.'

'Son.' The word was breathed, pained. Oxygen was dragged in. Out. In. Out. A conscious act, desperate. 'Got. Your. Way. In. The. End.'

'Dad, please don't start. I was trying to help. I didn't want you sitting for hours in a cold cubicle struggling to breathe until someone was free to see you. It's so much better here. See, you were admitted straight away. Whatever you want, just ask. I've got this.'

His dad didn't say anything, he didn't have to. He just turned his head away and closed his eyes. His silent comment: *I don't want anything from you.*

And right now Jake didn't care what his dad thought about being here. It was better than the public hospital and Bill Lewis deserved the best. But Jake understood that being there would put a dent in the old man's pride.

He picked up his dad's admission notes and scanned them. Blood pressure was erratic, blood gases were haywire, his lung function was severely compromised. This visit was just one of many he'd probably have over the next few years. COPD was a long, slow struggle of fighting infection and trying to halt further deterioration.

There was silence as everyone looked at their feet. It was so damned sad that they had nothing to say to each other at a time like this. He went for the mundane, to keep the peace. 'How's the house? Garden?'

His mom's face brightened at the distraction, a bit of normality. 'Oh, you know, same as always. I'd like to spruce the place up a bit, but…well…' She nodded towards his dad. 'You know…'

He did. The wallpaper in the dining room had been exactly the same all Jake's life, the carpet too—too much upheaval, they'd said, to change it all. Too much dust—and no respite for a man with damaged lungs. The dining suite must have been thirty years old, the upholstery fraying on the seats.

Jake nodded. 'Fresh air helps—if it's not too humid. How about trying to get outside? You've got that nice outdoor furniture—sit out a while.'

Mom shook her head. 'The garden's got away from us these days—it's too big to deal with.

And things grow so fast. I couldn't sit and look at that mess.'

'Then I'll come round and sort it out.' No excuses. 'You can sit out and feel the sun on your back.' She was too drawn and pale these days, looking after an obstinate man who put pride before any kind of enjoyment.

'That would be lovely, Jakey. Thank you. We were so looking forward to you coming for dinner today. Such a shame...' His mom's voice died away and silence fell again.

Meanwhile, Lola sat to his left, her hands in her lap, knees tight. She looked about as uncomfortable as Jake felt.

He checked the oxygen flow, read the heart monitor. Again. Pulse rate was fast but settling. Blood pressure a little lower than before. Sats still low but rising. 'So, Dad, how're you feeling now? That medicine doing its magic?'

'Can't. Complain. Son.' A shallow breath. Heaving chest. Another breath. But his skin was starting to pink up. 'How's that job?'

'Just fine.'

'Good.'

This was how it was. His father never commented on how he felt and they kept conversation to anything other than personal. He couldn't think of a single thing to say. No. Not right. He could think of a million things to say but they wouldn't listen.

He thought about his old home, the photos that lined the walls. Pictures of him when he was a little boy, high on his dad's shoulders. Of the three of them at a baseball game. Christmases. His birthdays. Of his graduation. In all of them they were smiling. So proud. Even though money had been woefully tight on the salaries of a part-time nurse aide and an untenured teacher, they'd been happy. A fist clamped tight round his heart. At what point had they gone from a unit of three to strangers? Would they ever get it back?

Was it too late?

'So he kicked towards me, grabbed me tight and swam hard to the beach.' Lola's voice brought him back—she was showing them her war wound. 'It was a plant, would you believe it? A plant can do that much harm?'

'There are a few plants you need to avoid in California that you may not have in London. Jake'll tell you all about poison oak. He once—'

'Not necessary to tell Lola all my secrets, Mom. Especially the ones that involve me being naked.' He turned to Lola. 'I was four at the time. We were camping.'

'Sounds painful. But I bet you were super-cute then.' She smiled. Heat flashed across her eyes and she swallowed, the glimmer of a private smile on her lips. Then her gaze caught his and the word 'naked' had stoked his memory. And he was surprised at the heat that flashed through him. Intense. Immediate. She turned back to his mom and dad. 'Well, he won't admit it, but I'd like to say he saved my life.'

His mom looked impressed. 'That's my Jakey.'

Lola nodded and smiled, knowing damned well he hadn't saved her life. He knew what she was doing, trying to make him out to be some kind of hero. It was a kind gesture. Smoothing things over, making light of them, her smile ready for everyone. She had an easy manner that seemed to cut through the tension. It had never occurred to him to bring any of his friends to meet them before. At first it had been due to—he was ashamed to realise now—embarrassment of the lowliness of his origins in comparison to those of the other medical students. Then anger had overshadowed the embarrassment. Then there had seemed little point, because there was nothing to say when he came.

Lola smiled at his mom. 'And you were a nurse, Mrs Lewis? Is that right? Is that why you decided to be a doctor, Jake? Following your mum's footsteps into medicine?'

'Oh, no.' His mom blushed and waved her hand in front of her face. 'Jakey was far too clever to follow me. We knew that from when he was a little boy. He did everything faster, better than the other kids. He was singled out at school. They have a name for it now, gifted and talented. But back then he was just top of the class in everything. His father used to give him extra lessons to keep him from getting bored.'

'That's enough about me, Mom. Thanks. We don't want to bore Lola to death.' But his mother wasn't listening.

'We don't see enough of him now, of course. He's so busy.'

'I know, Mom. I'm sorry.'

'Your…mother…misses…you.' It was the first thing his father had said for what felt like hours. It was a barb. It wasn't warm, like his mom's joking. It was a dart targeted at Jake's heart. And they both knew it. Staying away had been the way to avoid all the arguments, but it had made coming back all that much harder.

The temperature on the unit felt like it had plummeted. Things could go in one of two ways now, depending on how he handled this. He chose compliance. 'I know, I'm sorry, things get busy. I come when I can.'

'Not enough.' His father shook his head. 'You should come home more.'

'When you're better you could come to see me—a trip up to the city? Mom would like that. I could pick you up. It would be easy. You could get out of the house for a while.'

'What's wrong with the house?'

'Jake, I'm fine. It's fine. Bill, leave it. Please.' His mom's lip quivered, and just like that the tension spilled over.

'It's not fine, Deanna.' His father was shaking now, gulping air. 'Not at all.'

'There's nothing wrong with home, Dad. I just think it would be nice for you two to get out a little. We could take a drive. Have lunch out. Go to the ocean. Mom likes the ocean, remember?'

'I'm fine, Jake.' His mom's voice began to shake too. She'd always trod a fine line to keep the peace and made resolutely sure never to take sides. It must have been so hard for her. Every time. 'Please—leave it. Don't go upsetting your father.'

His dad's shoulders heaved up and down. 'Still…not seeing you means we…don't have to listen to all…those damned instructions…you bark at us. *Get a new car. Buy this. Change the kitchen. I'll buy that.* Like we can't manage.'

Lola stared down at her hands. Easy how things could go from hero to zero once he and his dad were in the same room.

'I'm sorry, Mom, Dad. I know I should let you be.' *Show gratitude*, Lola had said. 'I just want the best for you. I want you to know how grateful I am and that's the only way I can think of showing it.'

'Oh, Jakey, we know you're grateful. You don't have to do anything. Nothing at all.' His mom gave him a weary smile, popped her hand over his father's tight fist and waited until he'd relaxed a little. 'We're both so proud of you.'

And so he sat and tried to control the anger that was swirling inside him. And not to focus on the pain in his mom's eyes and the slump of her shoulders and the shabby coat. He tried hard not to notice the old shoes and the fraying hand-bag. He tried even harder not to listen to the rapid inhalation of his father's broken lungs, and tried not to think about all the things he could do to make their lives easier. If only they would listen.

Keep a lid on it. Gratitude. At the very least, be nice.

As they spent the next ten minutes chatting about nothing he focused on smiling and nodding at the conversation. He listened to Lola's attempts at jokes and he liked her even more for trying. Any other woman would have excused herself by now or thrown him *I want to leave* looks, but not Lola. She just carried on asking questions about his childhood as if there wasn't a thick cloud of doom hanging over them all, as if she didn't no-tice the dreariness and the atmosphere.

Gradually his father improved enough to take the mask off a little and, feeling reassured about his progress, Lola and his mother disappeared to get coffees. So Jake was left with his dad and the anger and the frustration, and he tried to suppress it. He wanted to try gratitude one more time, but the words wouldn't come because it wasn't their way. It wasn't how they did things.

He should have left it, buttoned his lip, but it was all too much for him to ignore. 'So, I get it that you have too much pride to use my money, Dad, and I know it's all just accumulating in some account somewhere and will all come back to me when you're both gone, just as you want. But look at Mom. Just look at her. She's tired, she's getting old, she needs a break. You both do. When was the last time you went on holiday?'

His father's face sagged with ill-concealed frustration. 'How can I go on holiday like this? Get real, Jake.'

He still tried to keep a lid on his temper, but it was wriggling loose at the edges, out of his grasp. 'It doesn't have to be hard. First class gets you decent help. I could hire a nurse. Two. Somewhere with great fishing. Mom could relax, and while you're away we'll organise some house renovations. Fresh paint, the garden—'

'For heaven's sake, Jake, how many times…?'

A little bit anger more wriggled loose, and he was just grateful Lola wasn't there to witness it. He tried to keep his voice quiet but, goddammit, sometimes it got loud. 'Hear me out, Dad. Please. I don't want you getting worked up. I know you don't want me to help, I know you say that providing all those years is a father's job, but it's a son's job too. How do you think I feel when I see you struggling? When I can help? When I can make things easier—if not on you then on Mom? I could organise a home-care nurse and give her a break…or just some housekeeping help. Doesn't *she* deserve a break?' They didn't need to be here, doing this. If his dad had better housing he wouldn't get so sick. If he got better treatment, these attacks would be fewer. If he'd sought help at the beginning… *If…if…damned if…*

His dad didn't have much time left and for the most part he could be well enough to travel—a short way, with help. They needed to be ticking things off a bucket list—or at the very least living in a place that wasn't making his condition worse.

'Dad, you remember when we went on vacation to Yosemite? D'you remember what fun we had? How much Mom laughed? You said you loved it when she did that. When was the last time you saw that?' And despite every attempt to keep it locked in, his anger finally wriggled free. He pressed his hand over his dad's, something he'd never done before. His dad's skin was paper thin, his fingers were frail and cold, but inside that man, Jake knew, there was a determined heart—it may have been damaged over the years and fighting to keep going, but it was full and proud. Hell, he'd gotten his grit from his father after all. 'Just stop being so damned stubborn. *Please.* You might not want to enjoy the last few years you have, but she deserves to. She wants to go out. She wants to have nice things. Stop trying to look after me. I don't need it. I'm all grown up now—it's my turn to look after you. I need to do this. You need to listen.'

There was a silence except for the rhythmic whirr of the oxygen cylinder, the irregular intake of breath. His father looked at him with dark sunken eyes, lines of ribs showed under his pyjama top, his thin wrists gripping the sides of his duvet. He looked and he kept on looking.

Jake looked right back. At the man who had

taught him how to ride a bike and how to fish, how to change a car tyre and how to put up a shelf straight. And then at what he'd been reduced to—for *him*. And the anger solidified into a hard physical lump in his chest. 'Oh, and just for the record, Dad, you don't get the monopoly on love either, you know. You don't get to make hard sacrifices for me without knowing this one thing; I'm very grateful. Really. I know I could never have got where I am without you, that's why I want to help. Why I *have* to help.' Jake took a wild leap. It was raw and angry but it was said. 'I love you, Dad.'

With that, Jake turned away. There was nothing more he could do or say. His throat was sore. His chest felt as if it was going to explode. He didn't know if it was enough—because how could words be enough after his father had sacrificed his health? But it was all Jake had—that and his repeated offers to be there for them if they needed him. That, after all, had been what he'd been trying to say for the last ten years through the anger and the fights. Just that. *I love you.*

And, damn it, just as Lola and his mom bustled back into the room, all polite smiles and coffee cups, he could have sworn he heard his father say, 'I know, son.' But he wasn't sure.

He didn't turn round to speak to them, he turned back to look at the man he'd adored with every childish breath. His eyes met his dad's again and they held. The older man's softened as Jake felt his soften. And he felt the strength of this once mighty man emanate from what was left of his broken body and pass to him. From father to son. A handing down, a rite of passage. A gift.

Nothing was said, but something gave. Finally. It wasn't a battle won, it was a war ended. 'Let's make it work, Dad,' he whispered, under the pretence of fixing the oxygen tubing.

And there, for a moment, was his dad's hand on his. A pat. Warmth in those bluish fingers and a fragile smile. The pride, though, his dad still had a good grip on that. *And so he should*, Jake thought. There was nothing wrong with being proud of what he'd achieved. 'Right you are, son. Starting now.'

Lola's hand was on his arm and she gave him a wary smile. He didn't know if she'd heard anything of what had been said between himself and his dad but she gave no indication of her thoughts.

'Jake, I hope you don't mind, but I've had a call. I need to get back to Bel Air.'

His heart was swollen but his mind was immediately on Cameron's pregnancy. 'Sure. Anything serious?'

'Depends on what you mean by serious. In her eyes, yes. She's a perfectionist and wants to get things right first take. She's got an important final shoot tomorrow and she wants to go over her lines,' Lola explained with a shrug. 'I should have said no. But I can't...I just...I'm so sorry. You know how it is. Work comes first.'

'But...' What was the point in arguing? He would take her to Bel Air and then come back here. End of. Although it was usually him breaking dates for emergencies. It was uncomfortable to feel it from the other side.

'I said I'd be there within the hour if possible.'

'Sure.' He was about to excuse himself from his parents, just for the time it'd take him to get her home.

But, as if she'd read his mind, she interrupted. 'No.'

Her gaze travelled from him to his dad and

back. 'You stay here. They need you here. I can make my own way.'

'I'll call you a cab at least. And—well, thank you.' He almost said more, but didn't. How could he? The fantasy he'd had about ending the day together in bed fizzled out. He'd wanted to show her his appreciation of how she'd helped him today—although that fantasy had also included him having a spectacularly great time too. It would have to wait until…until another time when they could both carve space out in their diaries.

One more night shoot and they'd have to work extra-hard at carving out that time because their paths wouldn't cross like they did on set. He'd be back to a full-time clinic and on-call roster. Cameron had already prepared him for the time-suck her pregnancy would be for Lola, at least in the short term. And with that and her work and her stubborn determination to win a battle only she was fighting, it would be hard to carve out anything meaningful.

In fact, if he looked at it rationally, her leaving now was a good thing—it meant they were both committed to the important things, they could sharpen their focus on their careers and consign this, whatever it was that they had, to a happy memory and not a distraction. And yet there was a strange twist in his chest at the thought of this coming to an end.

'Okay, Lola?'

'Yes, thanks. I've had a smashing day.' She gave him a sort of wobbly smile that meant she was sorry *but*…and he understood. Because work always did come first.

CHAPTER TWELVE

As soon as she walked into Cameron's house Lola was put on high alert. Her boss was more than a little tetchy as she paced up and down the family room, wringing her hands. Her usually perfect hair was a mess, there were black rings round her eyes, smudged lines of mascara down her cheeks.

'Cameron? Oh, my goodness, what's wrong?'

'Lola.' She didn't stop pacing. 'I thought you said you'd be back soon.'

'I came as quickly as I could. What is it? You look…well, you look dreadful.'

'It's this.' Cameron picked up her desert warrior dress from the sofa and threw it to Lola. Strange, because all costumes were meant to stay in the wardrobe trailer, not come home. Ever. Everyone knew the rules.

'Your dress? What's wrong with it? I know it's

a bit out there, but you've been fine about wearing it for the whole film.'

Cameron shook her head. 'It. Doesn't. Fit.'

'What? Where?'

'Everywhere.' Her boss sat down on the couch and worried her hands. 'I'm too big. All over.'

'That's okay, we'll get Maria to let it out. No big deal. I'll sort it, first thing in the morning.'

'She'll ask questions. I can't…' She ran her hand across her stomach and Lola looked closer. Her boobs were quite a bit bigger than normal. Her tummy was a little rounded. Cameron looked… well, apart from the make-up mess, she was glowing with health.

Holy. Moly. 'You're pregnant.'

'Yes.' Her voice was a tiny squeak. The healthy glow had given way to a little green around the lips. Pregnancy explained a lot—the strange diet, the mood swings, the broodiness. The need for a physician. 'What am I going to do?'

'What do you want to do?' Something twisted in Lola's gut. It wasn't jealousy as such. Or maybe it was. Lola hadn't given a thought to settling down and having a family, at least any time in the near or medium future, so she couldn't fathom why she should suddenly ache for a piece of that. Sympathy hormones, clearly. Get two women in the same room for any amount of time and their hormones fell into sync. She'd clearly been spending way too much time with Cameron.

With this crisis, that would only escalate.

'Keep it, I think. I don't know. The timing's all wrong. But…I didn't want to even think about it. I didn't want to be pregnant and it's taken me a lot of time to get used to the idea. And I have to fit into that dress. I have to wear nineteenth-century corsets and ride a damned horse in a month.' She took a quick breath and carried on, her words coming faster and faster. 'I think I felt it kick an hour ago. I don't know, maybe not, but there was something. A flutter. And now it all feels so real and I've been squishing it into this dress, pretending it wasn't happeni—'

'Stop it. Stop it, right now.' Lola stepped forward and took her boss's hands. She'd started to sound hysterical. 'Getting worked up won't be good for your baby. You have to be a mum now, responsible. Think about what it needs, not just what you need.' *That was probably going to be the hardest bit*, Lola thought. Then she caught herself—because when Cameron focused on a project she always did it to perfection. 'You'll be a great mum. You will.'

Her boss stared at her open-mouthed. Then nodded, slowly. 'Yes. Yes, of course. And I need to stay calm.'

'Exactly.' Although a little hysteria now would be nothing compared to the media furore when word of this got out. Lola would be on call night and day, and could kiss goodbye to any kind of personal life for a while. There would be journalists to deflect, speculation on the baby's gender, an army of paparazzi whenever Cameron went out. A barrage of baby and maternity wear and gifts that would arrive from companies across the world, wanting Cameron to endorse their brands, and they would need cataloguing and thank-you cards. OB/GYN appointments...tests. A different kind of gym workout. A new menu, probably a new chef who specialised in maternal nutrition. It might even be easier if she moved into Cameron's for a while.

And...who was the father? Wouldn't he want a say, wouldn't she have to co-ordinate diaries? Organise nannies and nurses and research the best diapers—because Cameron always wanted to be seen as eco-conscious because that got more headlines. Not counting private planes and carbon footprints, obviously.

It would be a terrible time for a PA to leave or to demand extra time for herself. Cameron needed her. It would be fine, Lola asserted. It would be okay. Busy, but okay.

'Look, Cameron, we'll work it all out. We'll sit down and make a list and go through it all one thing at a time. When you're ready. But first off I'll get out my sewing machine and let out your costume tonight—no one will know, we can say you accidentally left it in your trailer. Next thing; let's get you something to eat and drink—you need to feed the baby. Thirdly, you don't have to do *Hayley's Way.* You know, you are in charge of your career.' Lola didn't miss the irony of those words.

'Honey, that was my chance for Cannes. It was going to be my career-affirming film.'

'You're at the top of your field already, you couldn't be more career-affirmed. This has happened and now you just have to deal with it. Enjoy it. Carve out some time in your life… It is possible. You can do this. Now, let me make you a cup of mint tea. That'll help settle you. And a snack. We can talk. Think. Plan.'

This was a very strange end to her day. She couldn't have imagined when Jake had knocked on her door—

Jake.

She had that same twisting in her gut at the thought of him. If she'd thought that there might be time for any kind of fling then, that was now dead in the ground. There wasn't going to be any time for her to focus on herself, never mind him, or a relationship, and what guy would put up with that?

This was her life, this was her job, and it was a doorway to a much better place. She just needed to suck it up and do what Bill Lewis had done: make sacrifices, no matter how much they hurt. She had to step up for Cameron.

Oh, but before she did that there was one thing she would do for herself: she would call her family and confess. She would ask her father's opinion about her script. Then she would put her head down and work in what little spare time she could find. Which meant no Jake.

One day she'd be in a position to put the rest of her life first. To fall in love and have all the trimmings. One day she'd be in control of her timetable enough to have everything. Because that was what she'd have to deny herself to get to that point, everything that other people had—the house, the job, the guy.

One day she'd have time for someone significant. Someone she loved and who loved her right back. It wasn't a lot to ask, no wild or whacky dreams—she didn't want anything extraordinary. Something that Mr and Mrs Lewis had would be great. Better than great. A whole lifetime with one person—a life together, memories, children, a commitment.

With Jake?

She wasn't one hundred per cent sure, but she had a sneaking suspicion that the answer to that question was yes. One day. Just not today.

Or any time soon.

The dress fitted well after Lola's late-night alterations. Cameron was pleased that no one had questioned why the costume had disappeared overnight, and the shoot was almost complete.

Just a short break then the final lines would be said and the truly dreadful space-desert-odyssey would be a wrap.

Then they would be navigating uncharted territory: announcing the pregnancy and dealing with the fallout; renegotiating the *Hayley's Way* contract—a meeting with lawyers and Cameron's agent had been scheduled for tomorrow.

Lola just had to get through tonight. Seeing Jake. Telling him about having to refocus on her job…pregnancy talk would be strictly off limits. Cameron had made her swear utter secrecy.

Leaving Jake.

She glanced outside the trailer into the car lot and thought for a second that she could see him strolling towards her. But that was wishful thinking. Relief and dread threaded through her; it was madness to feel like this. To want a man so badly and to have to break things off.

She closed her eyes for a moment as a keen pain fisted in her chest. She'd found a good man. One who wanted her—at least, she thought he did. One who made her laugh, made her sigh, made her want things so out of reach. She had two options. She could do what her father did and commit to a relationship at the risk of everything else in his life. Or she could suggest a clean break, enjoy the memories and survive the heartache.

She knew without a shadow of a doubt that she wasn't her father.

Then she shut off all lines of thought because it was just too hard to keep thinking and rethinking, and seeing Jake's face in her mind's eye and remembering his touch and the way he made her feel.

'So! A great day's work today so far? A cup of tea, Cameron, while we're waiting? A smoothie?'

'Oh, you darling. Peppermint tea, please.'

'Of course!'

A snuffling at her feet had her looking down at the floor. Jelly clearly wanted some attention, so she bent to pat her and as she did so her hand brushed against Cameron's bag. There was a script there. Not unusual—Cameron was always working. But it wasn't the one Cameron was supposed to be reading… Lola's heart almost stopped. Then it started to thump loud and hard against her ribcage. *Her* script? How could Cameron have got hold of it? Had she seen it, *borrowed* it to read? Had she been going through Lola's things?

This was not okay. 'Er…excuse me, Cameron?'

'Yes, honey?' Her boss was propped up by satin cushions, snoozing, feet up on the couch after a hard hour or two's acting. She didn't usually like to be interrupted. But…*what the hell*?

'Sorry, but is that…is that…my script you're reading?' She could hardly say the words, her mouth was suddenly dry and thick.

'Why, yes, it is. Jake gave it to me the other day. He said it was good, but he was wrong…'

'Oh.' *Jake gave it to her? Jake gave it to her? And she hated it.*

The actress's eyes flickered open. She smiled. 'It wasn't good, Lola, it was great. I love it. In fact…' she patted the cushion next to her, inviting Lola to sit '… I'd like to option it.'

'Option it? But you don't have a production company.'

'I'm thinking of starting one after the baby comes. We have to diversify as we age, darling.'

Lola tried to control herself, because…well, Cameron was nothing but astute. She'd made a decent career for herself. She wanted to do something with Lola's script—out of all the scripts she saw month after month.

This was huge.

But Jake! What had he been thinking? Why the hell would he want to step in and take over, when he knew how she felt about being in control of her own life? Had anything she'd said meant anything to him?

'You know, Cameron… I'm not actually all that sure what I'm going to do with it yet. I wasn't going to show it to anyone for a little while. Not until I'd made sure it was finished. But…well… Wow. If you think it might work, that would be…' Lola stood and glanced out the window again. This time she did see Jake striding across the lot, wearing the same guarded expression he'd had last night. 'Sorry…got to go…I won't be long.'

Cameron sighed. 'Take the dogs—?'

Lola didn't have the wherewithal to listen to Cameron's next words. Her ears were burning with a raging white noise. She pulled the door closed, stormed down the steps, ignoring the tug in her heart just at the sight of him, and hissed, 'What on earth did you think you were doing? Showing Cameron my script? How dare you?'

'Good evening, Lola.' He stopped short, clearly understanding how important it was right now to keep his distance. 'You're going to have to help me out here because I was trying to do a good thing.'

'That is my script. That is my work. How dare you interfere? I will fashion my career when I'm ready, not when you think's a good time.'

'Hey, I thought it might give you a hand up. You're not exactly pushing yourself forward. I was trying to help. I believe in that script. And you, Lola. I believe in you.'

'I am sick of people thinking they know what's best for me. Okay? I will do things the way I want, when I want.' He was just like her parents. Would no one listen? 'Besides, I was waiting to hear what my dad said about it.'

His eyebrows rose. 'You told him? Everything?'

She took a deep breath. It would have been nice to share this in better circumstances but there it was. 'Yes. I did. He wasn't thrilled, neither of them were. It was difficult...there were tears... but it's now out in the open. He said they'd only wanted me to be happy, that I should have told them earlier. Most of all they were disappointed

I lied. I get that. I know I did the wrong thing, but I doubt they'd have been open to it before.'

'Feels better, right?' Jake reached out and smoothed his hand over her hair. 'Took some guts.'

It had taken great willpower, but she'd done it because she'd seen what a difference being honest had made to Jake and his father. It was a sound platform for them to develop something better. 'You bet it did.'

'I know it did.' He smiled. 'So he read it?'

'He emailed me this morning. He loves it…he's given me a couple of suggestions for changes. I wanted to make them before I showed it to anyone. Like…you know… Cameron? I can't believe you took my property and handed it over without asking my permission. That is unforgivable.'

'We can talk to her.' He seemed to realise his mistake immediately. 'Sorry, *you* can talk to her. Suggest you tweak it a little—ask her if she thinks it needs it. Tell her what you need.'

'To be honest, I'm not sure she'll care what I need right now, she's got other things on her mind.' In the background, underneath the noise in her ears and Jake's voice, Lola could hear barking. Lots of barking. She ignored it, raised her voice. 'Just this once I'm going to let Cameron deal with them.' She tugged him away from the trailer to a more deserted part of the lot. 'While I deal with you.'

He came willingly. *Annoyingly.* Because she wanted him to refuse, she wanted to drag him bodily across the tarmac and cause some serious damage to his lovely leather shoes. Just…well, just because.

She wanted to tell him that she was so damned angry that he'd overstepped the mark. And yet she still wanted him. That he caused too many emotions in her head. That her heart hurt every time she woke up without him. That he'd caused a tsunami of chaos in her life and had made her want so much more. So. Much. More. But she couldn't have it. She couldn't focus on what she needed to do, what she'd fought hard for, and give him what he deserved.

She wanted to tell him that of all the emotions he'd imprinted in her, the one that shone so brightly in the centre of her chest was something she was scared of. Scared because it was so huge, so important. So devastating. She wanted to tell him that…that she loved him.

Because surely that was what this was? She loved him. Needed him in her life. She ached to wake up with him. For him to be the last person she thought of every night. For them to have a future.

She closed her eyes. *Oh, God.* She loved him.

A sharp pain pierced her heart. How had that happened, when she'd tried to convince herself all along that she was in control of her own destiny? Loving Jake wasn't something she could do—not now. Not here. Not when everything was against them.

Which meant it wasn't going to be okay. It wasn't going to be okay at all.

He had the audacity to smile. 'So is this the part where we kiss and make up?'

'No, Jake.' And she started to shake. 'This is the part where it ends.'

Jake looked at her—at the way she was standing, hands on hips, trembling with anger, a flashback to the first day he'd met her, which seemed like a lifetime ago and yet was only a matter of weeks. And yet so much had changed. So much that he'd had to work through. More than one sleepless night. But most noticeably, last night, when he'd gone to bed with a definite plan of ending it. It was too complicated. Too hard in a world when clambering to the top of a career was tough enough.

But he'd woken up with such a need to see her that he couldn't bring himself to conjure up the words. And the moment he'd laid eyes on her again and felt the lift in his heart he'd known that this wasn't something ordinary. This was the most special thing he'd ever had. And now she was throwing it away because he'd done something lame. To her way of thinking. In his, he'd been doing a darned good thing.

And now here she was, saying the words he'd practised and then dismissed, because he believed in what they had. Believed they had a future if they were prepared to work towards it together.

He looked into the intense brown eyes that were raging with emotions—so many he couldn't keep up. Anger—yes, there was a lot of that. And desire—that was there too. A little bit of humility and embarrassment. And something else. Something that he connected with so profoundly it stripped the breath from his lungs—so he couldn't work out why her words and her eyes didn't match. 'You want to end it?'

'Yes.'

'Because I gave Cameron your script?'

She frowned. 'No. Don't be stupid. That's not a valid reason. Although I am fuming about that. Really bloody angry.'

'Yes. You are. I can see and I'm sorry. But if it's not because of that, then why? Why does it have to end?'

'Because it isn't a great time for me right now. There's too much at stake for me to get distracted by something that may come to an end…I can't risk the rest of my life on you.' Here her voice cracked. 'I'm sorry, Jake. We said in Nassau that it was short term. Just for fun. We've got to…just stick by that.'

'Things can change, Lola. We can change with them. Hell, it's up to us what we do.'

She shook her head vehemently. 'But that's where you're wrong. Your career is established but you still have to do things that interfere with it—like the trip to the Bahamas. Like working here—you didn't want to do it. It was out of your control. But for me, I'm striving here, I have a plan and I need to follow it.'

'And that doesn't include me.'

'No. I'm sorry.' She glanced back towards the trailer, where the barking was continuing, as if to prove her point. Cameron was useless without someone to run her life. He got that. But it didn't have to be all-consuming, did it? Lola shrugged. 'We have too much to do, too much to create for ourselves before we can commit to settling down. There's just too much. I can't do it all— I'm so tired. It's exhausting trying to sleep and think and feel all these things for you. And then keep on working all hours and write and edit... and still keep on feeling these things.'

He tried to cajole her. Made a joke. 'You could take a leaf out of my book and learn how to juggle a bit better—if it's good for the brain, it might work for the heart too.'

'Not right now, Jake. I'm sorry.' The corners of her mouth lifted. 'And Cameron needs me. There's...things happening.'

She knows Cameron's pregnant. She knows but she can't say. And neither could he—because he couldn't take the risk. If he mentioned it first he'd be blowing all confidentiality and that would risk harming the clinic's reputation, his job…her work. Her damned plan.

It seemed everything came down to that.

But it wasn't insurmountable. 'Other people manage to have relationships and work hard. Plenty.'

'And many don't. Relationships suffer or someone has to compromise—like my dad did. Give up a dream. Regret. *God*, I don't want that to happen. I don't want to look at my kids with that in my eyes. That would break my heart…'

He already felt as if his already had. 'Don't I get a say in any of this? What about what I want? What if I think it can work? What if I say I want it to?'

She reached her hand to his chest and laid her palm there. 'One day. One day we'll both be in the right space to do this.'

'What? You'll call me? You'll call and say, *Hey, I'm ready now*? And you think I'll come running? When? A year? Five? Ten? You think this is going to stay in here?' He pointed to his heart and, yes, he knew he'd still feel these things for her in a year, two, a decade. His heart felt blown open, raw. She'd taught him how to live again and now she wanted to cut off his damned oxygen. He wanted to fight, wanted to grab her and talk sense in to her. But this impossibly positive woman didn't think it would work. And if she didn't think it would work—if she couldn't make it work by infusing everything with a zillion of her jolly exclamation points—then they were certainly totally doomed. 'You want to take a chance on that? On us both being in the right space at the right time some time in the future?'

'It's all I've got, Jake.' She had to raise her voice a little, as the barking was louder now. She took two steps away from him. Might well have been a hundred. 'I'm sorry, I really think I'd better go and see what's happening—'

'Go to Cameron. Figures.'

'Jake, I've got to—'

'You want to prioritise a job you don't even want over a relationship? It doesn't add up, Lola. You're not making sense.' She was about to argue back, he could see, but he rattled on. Unable to stop. 'What the hell are you scared of?'

She was defiant, chin in the air. 'Scared? I'm

not scared. You just don't understand what it's like to finally start to live a life you want, instead of moulding yourself on someone else's dream.'

'Are you really saying I don't know what it's like to have parents who have poured their whole lives into yours? Really? You saw my father, Lola. I live with that every single day.'

Her hands fisted at her sides. Tears pricked her eyes but she blinked them away. 'I'm saying you don't know what it's like to fight your way out of that. It was suffocating. Too much pressure. Too much living someone else's life. I need to live my own life. I need to know that I can make it. On my own.'

'And that doesn't include compromise? Or falling in love? Or taking a risk? Not a great life, Lola.'

'Right now it's the best I can do. I'm not afraid to make hard choices. I'm sorry, Jake. So sorry.' She turned to leave but he grabbed her wrist, pulled her to him and felt the tight press of her body against his. The way her bones moulded against his, the way her eyes told him of the way she truly felt and the way her mouth said words he didn't want to hear.

So he did the only thing that made sense and he cut the words off. He slammed his mouth over hers and kissed her with everything he had. For a moment she kissed him back with just the same amount of force. But then she pulled away. Her eyes were filled with tears and she put a hand to her mouth as if holding in a cry. Then she swallowed and shook her head. 'Jake, I can't. I want to. But I can't.'

With that she turned and ran back towards the trailer.

Jake shoved his hands into his pockets. Walked back towards the set where Alfredo gave him a warm smile and indicated for him to sit and watch them inch towards the final take of the worst movie in living history. And in his chest a fist of darkness tightened. He'd lost her. Lost her to this crazy life where nothing was real, where nothing made sense—not least his raging emotions. And there was absolutely nothing he could do about it. He felt like a raw exposed nerve. A damned artery, leaking hope, that he couldn't cauterise.

'*A-a-a-nd* action!' Alfredo called, and silence descended across the fake lunarscape. The leading man started to crawl across the floor, maimed and injured after a supposed alien attack. But the set of his jaw told the hushed audience that he would rise again and fight back.

Jake almost laughed. *Go on, man. Fight for all you're worth. Sometimes you just can't win, no matter what you do.*

Then out of the silence rose a terrified cry. Then another. And his heart began to drum. Because it wasn't on set, it was out in the car lot.

It was Lola, screaming his name.

CHAPTER THIRTEEN

HE RAN TO HER, doctor's bag in hand, the echo of his fast-beating heart drumming in his ears. She was standing at the top of the trailer steps, chest heaving as she smothered a sob. And he wanted to scoop her up, to kiss those cheeks pink again. But she held her hand up, keeping him at a distance, as if touching him would break her.

There was blood on her palms.

'What the hell…? Lola, what's happened?'

'Cameron…' She shook her head but motioned for him to come inside. There, on the floor, was the actress lying in a heap. She was moaning, pale. Blood on her forehead.

And her skirt.

The baby.

Head injury and threatened miscarriage. Potential brain bleed. Loss of blood.

The dogs were yelping around her, licking her face, running in circles.

Jake focused. 'Lola, get them out of here. They're going to get in the way. And call the clinic. Now. Get them to send the helicopter. Immediately.'

'Absolutely.' She took the dogs outside and he heard her on her cell phone. Her voice was surprisingly calm, compared to the chalk white panic of her face.

He knelt at Cameron's side and felt her pulse as he spoke gently. 'Cameron? Cameron. Hey…' Her eyelids flickered open and she opened her mouth to speak, but her face crumpled. 'It's okay…it's okay. Just lie here, it's okay. I'm going to ask you some questions. I'm going to need you to tell me a few things.'

She nodded, then closed her eyes again. Her hand was on her abdomen. But the blood loss appeared worse on her head, so he dealt with that first. He rummaged in his bag for his blood-pressure monitor. 'How did you end up down here?'

'Fell. Dogs.'

'You fell over the dogs?' No surprise there.

She nodded weakly. Her trembling hand went to the bump on her head. At first glance it looked superficial. Just a gash that was bleeding heavily.

But that didn't mean there wasn't deeper damage. He cradled her head in his hands, keeping it still, and checked the depth of the wound, the size of the lump. Clearly no neck or spinal damage as she was moving all limbs. 'You took a nasty knock there. What did you hit it on, can you remember?'

'Table.'

'You fell over the dogs and hit your head on the table?' He assumed it had been the corner judging by the jagged edge of the laceration. But she was showing no memory loss. 'Did you black out?'

'No. I don't think so.'

'You know where you are?'

'On the floor, honey, and it's sticky.'

At least her sense of humour was intact. 'In? Location?'

'West LA. Film set.' She sounded groggy, her limbs heavy as he tested her reflexes and her pupil reactions. All normal. He'd do a full concussion check once they were at the clinic. Signs of concussion or something worse might not show for a few hours.

'And now here?' He placed his hand softly against the tiny pregnancy bump. The blood on her skirt didn't appear to be getting any worse. 'How does this feel?'

A single tear edged down her cheek. 'Hurts.'

Lola tiptoed back into the trailer. 'ETA five minutes. They can land over in the far car lot. I've okayed that with security. But you need to know something, Jake… She's…' Lola worried her bottom lip with her teeth, then sighed. 'I'm sorry, Cameron, I'm going to have to tell him—'

'Pregnant.' He held Lola's gaze and she gave him a faint smile of acknowledgement. 'I know. I've known for a while.'

'Of course you have.' She knelt and took her boss's hand. 'Cameron, it's going to be okay. Jake will take care of you.'

Blood pressure low, but not dangerous. Yet. At least that was something, but her pulse was racing. He looked at Lola and they both looked at the spotting on Cameron's white skirt. He needed to assess just how much blood she was losing. 'Cameron, I need to examine your abdomen to check on the baby. Is that okay? And I need to know how much blood loss there is. Do you want to lie on a couch?'

'No. Here.' The actress shuddered on a sob,

but nodded. Lola fetched some towels, then held Cameron's hand while he assessed the size of the uterus and checked for tenderness and further blood loss. 'This isn't exactly a great place for doing this. We need to get you to the clinic and get you checked out.'

'But...the film.'

'This is more important. I'll talk to Alfredo.'

Lola nodded. 'I just have. He's fine. He wants me to let him know how you are. Later.' She stroked her employer's hair back away from the cut and then held the gauze Jake gave her over it to stem the bleeding.

He watched her as she chatted away, gently soothing. He imagined if the tables were turned and it were Lola lying on the floor. Cameron would be a mess.

Lola caught his gaze and held it for a few seconds. Underneath the reassuring noises she was pale and spooked, he could see that, but she was strong and holding everything together. As she looked at him her eyes softened and she bit her wobbling lip.

Pain ripped through him. After this he wouldn't see Lola again. He couldn't imagine that. Didn't

want to think about it. Didn't want to acknowl-
edge the emotion that was lodged in his throat as
he watched her. So he turned away and focused
on his patient. 'I'm just going to take your blood
pressure again, Cameron.'

Her hand grasped his. 'Please. Don't let me lose
this baby. Please. I—I wasn't ready, but I am now.
I'm ready for this. Don't let me lose it. So precious...'

'He won't,' Lola whispered to her boss, but she
stared right at Jake—her eyes boring into him
with such belief and hope that he didn't deserve.
'He won't let you lose this baby.'

Cameron's fingers gripped white on his as she
finally realised what she had and what she was
at risk of losing. But their faith in him was too
damned high. He closed his eyes. Because, really, it was out of his hands. He could monitor her
blood pressure and give her IV fluids when the
paramedics arrived. He could treat her as best he
could in the helicopter, but he couldn't promise
anything, not where a baby was concerned. He
was a neurosurgeon, not a gynaecologist.

Then the air was filled with the sound of chopper blades and he told Lola to go out and bring the

paramedics over. And he tried to keep his patient as reassured as best he possibly could.

When the team had safely got Cameron onto a stretcher with an IV line in situ and she was haemodynamically stable for now, he helped them down the steps and over the tarmac.

Lola stood, arms wrapped around her chest as she watched them load the stretcher into the helicopter. Her face was bleak, haunted. Sad. It took everything he had not to bundle her to him, but she'd drawn a line and he had to respect that. One stolen kiss was probably a step too far already. 'She'll be okay, Lola.'

She looked at him with black-rimmed eyes. 'How can you be sure?'

'She'll be fine. Go with her. In the chopper. Go.'

The trembling from earlier was back. 'No. You go. You're the doctor, you'll know what to do. I'll be useless.'

He took hold of her hands. 'She needs *you*.'

'No, she doesn't.' Her head shook. 'Go, Jake. I'll drop the dogs at home with the housekeeper. I shouldn't have brought them here in the first place but she went on and on about wanting her babies with her. I knew it was a stupid idea. I shouldn't have left her with them.'

'Lola. Stop it. None of this is your fault.'

'How can you say that?'

'Because accidents happen. Don't beat yourself up about this. You did not cause this.' The irony of the words haunted him and for the first time he realised that he was not responsible for his father's illness. There could have been many reasons why he'd got so sick and why he hadn't asked for help in the early stages—and only some of them were about his son. The rest were about his father's stubbornness, about the arbitrary nature of life. How some people could bounce back from infection and others needed adjunct therapy. How some people survived surgery and others didn't. How you met someone who had a profound effect on your life and because...*because* they're made like you, it seemed impossible that either of you could find space to make it work.

Wide eyes peered up at him beneath a frown. 'If we hadn't been outside... If I'd come back in as soon as I heard the dogs... Jake, what if she loses the baby?'

'You can't live your life on ifs, Lola. We'll do

everything we can to make sure that doesn't happen. Now, go. Do what you need to do with the dogs and meet me at the clinic.'

'Save her, Jake.'

'I'll try.'

She gave him the first smile he'd seen from her in hours. 'Oh, I have faith in you.'

'Do you?' He couldn't help but feel pain at that laughable statement. 'In my skills, yes. But nothing else.'

'What do you mean? Of course I have faith in your skills. You're an amazing doctor.'

He wanted her. Wanted to hear more than that from her, because she was deluding herself if she thought they could put some kind of halt to the way they felt about each other. Love wasn't something you could put on hold until you decided you wanted it—it burned into you like a brand.

Love.

Yeah. So there it was. He loved her.

At this revelation his heart skipped a couple of beats, and he felt the space in his chest implode, then it thudded back to a sorta, kinda sinus rhythm. The same but different—just like he was, having met Lola. The same guy with the same goals, but changed. Irrevocably.

It was a fine time to realise this as the chopper's blades began to whir and his work called to him—and she was walking away. It was the second time in two days he'd thought about how much he loved someone—and thought about telling them. This time, though, he'd keep it to himself. She didn't need to know how he felt.

He didn't want to admit it, but the thought of loving and losing Lola was just too damned hard. 'And there I was thinking that we make a great team. You know what's better than being on your own? Someone who can work *with* you, like we just did. A champion. Someone who believes in you more than you believe in yourself. Who's there to pick you up when you need it. Like you did with me and my dad. Like I did when you were sick. We make a good team, Lola—we could be brilliant together. I would never stand in the way of your dreams but, hell, I'd cheer you on. Anywhere. Everywhere. I'd support you, I'd carry you when you needed it and I'd stand back to let you shine in your own way too.'

'I know you would.' Her lip began to tremble. 'I know.'

'So here's what I don't get about this—you say you trust me enough to look after the life of your employer and her unborn child. You trust that I will make things right with my parents—that I will strive to look after them, whatever happens. You trust me to keep everyone safe. Except you.' He could see the pain in his heart mirrored on her face, but he didn't have time to make things right with her, or to convince her that he even could. He started to walk towards the chopper, the rush from the rotating blades blasting his words away as he turned around to look at her one last time. 'Why can't you trust me with your heart too?'

Lola drove way faster than the speed limit—and she didn't really care—along the narrow, winding roads towards The Hollywood Hills Clinic, heaving the car to the side every few minutes to allow yet another tourist bus to scrape past. Hundreds of people trying to catch a glimpse of a celebrity in the big houses flanking the road. No wonder the tarmac was in such a bad condition. She bumped in and out of potholes, each pause adding time to her journey. None of this mattered, of course. Only Cameron and the baby's safety.

And Jake.

His words resonated in her the whole trip. Had she been fooling herself that all this time she had been hiding behind her own dreams, when the real reason she'd held him off had been because she'd just been too scared to trust him?

Did she love him, truly? And what would that mean for her? For him? Could they make it work?

Bill and Deanna Lewis had found time for each other despite a child to care for, conflicting shifts and working all hours. The love between them had been right there, almost tangible. And her father had made a sacrifice for love; even though he'd chosen to move to London, she had no doubt he had made that choice willingly. Because there was a better thing than blindly following a career. A better thing than being totally alone just to prove a point, just to be able to say, *I am an independent person*. There was that thing called love that made everything just that little bit better.

What was the point in carving out a life for yourself if you had no one to share it? She'd be damned lonely in that studio apartment with just a script for company.

What if she lost Jake? That was just too much to contemplate.

She all but threw her car keys at the valet and ran into the impressive white building, and was greeted by soothing music, a water feature in the lobby and a smartly dressed, smiling receptionist at the front desk, with 'Stephanie' on her name badge. They'd bypassed this when she'd come here the other day to see Bill Lewis.

The calm that Jake usually emanated was right here in this place under the Hollywood sign, up in the hills. A far cry from the turbulent darkness in his eyes, the harsh anger as he'd spoken those last words to her. And her heart pounded even more. Not for Cameron this time, but for herself. Was it too late?

'Hi! I'm looking for Dr Lewis. Jake. And…' Lola leant forward so that the conversation would be private. Not that there were many people around, but confidentiality was king for Cameron. 'Cameron Fontaine?'

Stephanie smiled. 'Oh…er…I'll page Dr Lewis. Is he expecting you?'

'Yes. Tell him Lola's here.' She didn't press the point about Cameron…she'd hear soon enough from either the actress herself or Jake. The worse part was waiting, being the one who was excluded. The one who'd have to pick up the pieces. If…

She didn't want to think about it. 'I'm ready…' Cameron had said. She'd taken a huge step and for the first time in her life wanted something more than herself. Cameron knew just how much would change, it would have to—but she was going to do it. She was embracing it—and even though it would be a struggle, Lola hoped that Cameron would successfully manage thinking for two people.

Her boss was a whole lot braver than she herself was. Because right up until he'd mentioned trust, she hadn't been brave enough to let someone have a piece of her heart, or to allow herself to think about sharing her life.

But now…

It took him less than five minutes to appear in the lobby, but in that time she'd managed to control her heartbeat and take in some of the beautiful artworks on the wall, tried to allow the sound of the tinkling water to calm her nerves. She couldn't gauge his emotion as he walked towards her.

She couldn't gauge her own. Because, damn it, despite the words she'd said to him she was still not feeling the sentiment of them. Every part of her body ached to touch him, to feel his touch. She couldn't walk away. It made no sense. Being with Jake was the only thing that was clear.

But would he still want her after everything she had said?

He was wearing a white coat with the requisite stethoscope around his neck, and looked every inch like the dashing doctor in a starring role. 'Lola.'

'Hey, Jake.' And she felt like the villain. She didn't want to be anything other than herself, and right now she didn't feel the bright optimistic front she usually wore. She felt sad. Deflated. Anxious. Lost. Beaten. 'How's Cameron doing?'

He reached a hand to her arm and squeezed. His heat rushed through her and she saw kindness in his eyes. And...she dared to hope...something else. 'Cameron's being assessed by our obstetric team. She's in good hands.'

'And her head?'

'In the scheme of things it's not serious. Head wounds bleed. A lot. But she doesn't appear to have done any major damage. She's going to have a headache for a few days, but we'll keep an eye on all that along with the baby. One good thing, they were scanning as I left and I heard a heartbeat…'

'Thank God for that.' Lola closed her eyes and breathed out heavily, her hand on her chest. When she opened her eyes he was still there, his expression still unreadable. 'No, actually, thank you. Thank you.'

He shrugged. 'So. I'll take you to the family room and you can wait there. I have things to do.'

'Actually, wait. Can I talk to you? Maybe outside? I need some air.' She had no idea what she was going to say, or how to say it. Or even if he'd listen. But she wanted to tell him that she wanted to try. To be two. To be together.

'Sure. Whatever you want, Lola.' He started to lead her through the automatic doors and into the afternoon sunshine. 'If it's about your script again, I'm still sorry. I shouldn't have done it. I've learnt my lesson, I won't be looking to help again. You're on your own from now on. That's what you want, right?'

No. She wanted him. 'I don't know what Cameron will want to do with the script now. I have to bide my time, but she'll do right by me, I'm sure.'

'Good. It needs a home. It'll make a damn fine movie.' His eyebrows rose. 'So, what do you want to talk about?'

'Us.'

He came to halt. 'You made it very clear that—'

'I love you.' It wasn't exactly finessed, but it got the point over. It certainly shut him up.

'Oh.' He blinked, looking momentarily as lost as she was. 'I see.'

'And I want to share my life with you. At least, commit to each other. Something. Something important. Something mind-blowingly amazing. I don't know why I was so determined not to make a go of things, why I ended it so quickly. I think… You were right. I was scared by how much you mean to me. You grew on me pretty quickly and I was rattled by that. I didn't expect that it could feel so good…so, yes, I'm scared. Scared of throwing away everything I've worked so hard for. Scared that part of me would get lost a little in the concept of us, but scared even more about what I'll miss out on if I don't take that chance. I didn't mean to hurt you, Jake. I just couldn't figure out how we could love each other and keep that love alive in the midst of two very busy careers.'

'As I said before, lots of people do it. They make it work. We could have.'

'We still could. Make each other a priority. Really. I couldn't think of anything I'd like more than to see you in every spare moment I have. And I'll make more. Loads more. I'll speak to Cameron and ensure we stick strictly to the contract. If everything works out with the baby, I'll make her hire a nanny, two. Three. One each for the dogs… If everything works out with the screenplay I won't have to work for her at all…'

'Lola.' He paced in front of her, his logical brain clearly dealing with how to say no, gently. His directness was lost. She loved that about him. That he was clear-headed about everything but her. 'You made it clear that things were over. And now you come back here and hit me with this? What am I supposed to think now? Or to feel?

It's crazy. You're crazy. I don't want to hear any of this.'

'Oh.' Her throat stung. It was too late. She didn't know what to do now. She'd been so sure he wanted her. That her love for him would convince him. That they'd make it work. She'd been so sure. She stood for a moment and let the reality seep into her bones, into her heart. She'd lost him. Had been too cautious and had treated him badly. She allowed herself one last look at his deep blue eyes and his impossibly beautiful mouth. Then she hauled up every bit of strength she had, dug deep for the optimistic Lola he seemed to like. 'Okay! That's okay! It's fine! Really! I'll just go and find Cameron, see if she needs anything...' She turned and began to walk away.

She would not cry. She fought against the pain and a rising sob. Pressed a hand to her mouth. She would not cry.

'I mean, Lola, I don't want to hear another word because...' He pulled her close and kissed her hard on the mouth. Kissed her until her bones began to melt and her legs turned a little to jelly— or Jell-O, or whatever. They were wobbly, and her heart began to race. In a good way. A very good way. He kissed her until she was in no doubt as to how he felt. When he pulled away he was as breathless as her. 'I love you, Lola Bennett. And—strangely—I love your weird world of doggy danger and space-desert odysseys. And wildly demanding actresses and private planes and personal chefs. Of passion and dreams so beyond reach, and yet within grasp if you believe. Anything's possible. It's beyond bizarre. But I love it.'

'Things may get worse...I have a wild idea for my next screenplay. You may not like it, but I want to diversify. Cameron says we all should.'

He frowned. 'What could be worse than the princess-space-desert odyssey I've just lived through?'

'Zombie apocalypse?'

'Of course. That makes perfect sense.' He tipped his head back and laughed. 'Man, this is a crazy city. Bring it on. I love you, Lola Bennett, and your crazy life, and I want to share it. But mine might be a little dull in comparison.'

'There is nothing dull about your life at all— look at all those people you save, with just chopsticks.' She smiled, wondering how she'd ever thought she would have a complete life without him in it. 'And the passion with which you love people—so much it hurts—but you try to hide it. I love the things you do for me. You give me hope, you give me love, you give me wings. I love you right back.'

He kissed the tip of her nose and looked up at the Hollywood sign way up on the hill. 'Is this where we cue the soppy romantic music or the waves crashing on a beach?'

'No.' She took hold of the lapels of his white coat and tiptoed up to him. 'This is where you kiss me all over again.'

'Oh, I can do that. My pleasure. Over and over and over again.' He lowered his voice and his mouth, '*A-a-a-nd* action!'

* * * * *

Look out for the next great story in
THE HOLLYWOOD HILLS CLINIC
8 book series
PERFECT RIVALS... by Amy Ruttan

And if you missed where it all started, check out
SEDUCED BY THE HEART SURGEON
by Carol Marinelli
FALLING FOR THE SINGLE DAD
by Emily Forbes

All available now!
And there are four more fabulous stories
to come...